Victoria's hand to stomach fleetingly.

"You still haven't told your aunts." It wasn't a question.

"Don't," she begged quietly, and when it seemed Ben would argue, she turned her attention to Mikey. "Very nice," she encouraged, hugging his tiny body close for a second before he wiggled away.

"C'n I ski?" he asked suddenly. "'Cause a boy in church tole me he skis with other kids an' he 'vited me. Maybe he could be my friend?" he said wistfully.

"What a good idea." Victoria looked at Ben and found him studying her with an intensity that made her uncomfortable. "Don't you think?" she prodded.

"Uh, yeah. Skiing. Sure." Ben's gaze held hers for a second, then settled on Mikey. "We could do that, I guess."

Mikey ran around the room, cheering. Victoria stayed put, staring at her hands, unsettled by the expression she'd seen on Ben's face and her response to it.

He was a great guy. She liked him a lot. But there could be nothing between them but friendship. She was going to be a mom.

And soon Ben would leave.

Lois Richer loves traveling, swimming and quilting, but mostly she loves writing stories that show God's boundless love for His precious children. As she says, "His love never changes or gives up. It's always waiting for me. My stories feature imperfect characters learning that love doesn't mean attaining perfection. Love is about keeping on keeping on." You can contact Lois via email, loisricher@gmail.com, or on Facebook (loisricherauthor).

Books by Lois Richer

Love Inspired

Rocky Mountain Haven

Meant-to-Be Baby

Wranglers Ranch

The Rancher's Family Wish
Her Christmas Family Wish
The Cowboy's Easter Family Wish
The Twins' Family Wish

Family Ties

A Dad for Her Twins
Rancher Daddy
Gift-Wrapped Family
Accidental Dad

Visit the Author Profile page at Harlequin.com for more titles.

Meant-to-Be Baby

Lois Richer

ISBN-13: 978-1-335-42825-7

Meant-to-Be Baby

This edition published by arrangement with Love Inspired Books.

www.Harlequin.com

Printed in U.S.A.

And we know that all things work together for good to them who love God, to them who are the called according to his purpose.

—*Romans* 8:28

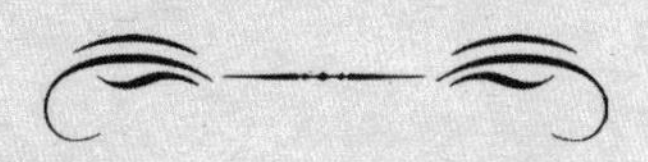

This book is dedicated to Dorothea,
who always believed God would make a way.

Chapter One

"We have to do something." Victoria Archer cradled her mug against her cheek and surveyed her two younger foster sisters. "*This time*, we were able to run home in time to help Aunt Tillie and Margaret clean up from that burst pipe. But what happens if—*when*—they have another emergency and none of us can make it back so fast?"

"It is January in the Canadian Rockies," Adele agreed in a gloomy tone. "And they're predicting a storm. If the aunties had an accident—"

"Or got sick." The awful thought silenced Olivia for a moment. "So what do we do?"

"I need to think about it." Victoria rose. "I'm going for a walk."

"Still proving you're tough enough to take whatever comes, huh?" Olivia shook her head. "Even the weather, Vic?"

"I always think better when I walk," Victoria defended.

"Wait. How'd you get here so fast, Victoria?" Adele studied her intently. "You live in Vancouver. When we spoke two days ago, you were settling some issue with a hotel in Toronto. Suddenly today you're here."

Time for the truth.

"Toronto was a simple fix and my last job with Strenga Hotels. I've taken a leave of absence from them. And Derek. He and I broke up." She hurried on. "I don't want to talk about *that* except to say that I'm now free to stay here at The Haven to help the aunts."

Avoiding their compassionate looks, Victoria pulled her gear off a wall hook: a white parka with a fur-trimmed hood, a thick red scarf, warm double-knit red mittens and knee-high insulated boots. Once dressed, she whistled for Spot and Dot, the two springer spaniels her foster aunts had rescued from a puppy mill three years ago. A glance at her sisters' worried faces made her smile.

"I really am okay. How about some of your scrumptious chicken potpie for supper, Chef Adele?" she suggested as she grasped the doorknob, eager to escape their pity.

"Perfect for a stormy day." Her sister began pulling out ingredients. "Be careful, Sis."

"Always. See you later." Victoria tucked her cell phone in her pocket and switched on the outside lights before leaving the big stone manor by the back door. The glow of the antique lanterns around The Haven chased away late afternoon shadows and lit a corresponding warmth inside her.

Home. Exhilaration bumped up her heart rate. Home. No Derek to consider. No pressing issue to tear her away from this glorious place. Well, there was that one huge issue looming…

The buffeting wind and whirling snowflakes turned the mountain foothills into a massive snow globe and ended her doubts. She loved The Haven. Her foster aunts' huge estate encompassed their massive stone home and acres of foothills and forest with the majestic tips of the Canadian Rocky Mountains in the distance.

Victoria smiled as the dogs bounded through the snowbanks, in and out of the spruce trees lining the driveway, chasing each other in circles but always returning to check on her before racing off again.

Yet despite the beauty surrounding her, thoughts of the future plagued Victoria. At the moment, her only certainty was that she would not return to the hotel chain that had employed her for five years. Her leave of absence would be permanent. There was nothing and no one there for her anymore. Derek had made that perfectly clear when she told him she was pregnant with his child.

"You're the famous fixer, Victoria. You've built a reputation in the hotel business by resolving issues with unhappy guests, broken reservation systems, under-functioning staff and a whole lot more. So handle this. Without me."

And when Victoria said she was keeping the baby, he'd dumped her. It took Derek less than a week to find a new romantic love.

So be it. Now her future would include single motherhood.

Scared, ashamed, embarrassed, worried—those emotions didn't begin to cover her wildly swinging feelings. But they weren't all negative. Wonder, amazement, a secret inner—was joy the right word to describe how amazed she was by the thought of becoming a mom?

Unable to make sense of her topsy-turvy reactions and still unsure of how she was going to support herself and her child, Victoria's thoughts veered to the immediate problem. What to do about the aunts. Moving Tillie and Margaret from The Haven, the home where they'd lived since retiring from the mission field twenty-five years ago, away from the friends they cherished and the land they adored—it was unthinkable. But how could they stay?

Lost in thought, Victoria finally roused to the dogs' frenzied barking. When they didn't return despite repeated calls, she knew something was wrong. She stopped to listen, trying to pinpoint their yelps through the whistling wind.

Over there. She climbed a steep hill, reached the summit, gazed around her and then caught her breath. The dogs stood guard beside—a child?

While she descended the hill, Victoria tried to fathom out the situation. She saw no adult, no vehicle, nothing to indicate where the child had come from. When she got closer, she realized the child was a young boy, and he was crying.

"Hello," she asked, squatting beside him. "I'm Victoria. Are you hurt?"

"Those dogs bited me," he sobbed and held up his arm to show her a tiny tear in the fabric of his snowsuit. "They won't let me help Unca Ben."

Victoria rose, searched the snowy scape before her but saw nothing.

"Where is Uncle Ben, sweetie?" she asked, trying to conceal her concern.

"Over there. He got hurted." The child pointed to the roadside but still Victoria saw only mounds of snow.

"What's your name?"

"Mikey," he sniffed and rubbed one mitten over his tear-covered cheek. "Those bad dogs won't let me help Unca Ben. They bited me," he repeated angrily.

"They were only trying to keep you safe. Spot and Dot won't hurt you." He clearly didn't believe her so Victoria sought to ease his fear by grasping his hand. "We want to help you and Uncle Ben, but I can't see him. Can you show me where he is?"

Mikey glared at the dogs so she gave a command. Immediately they sat and waited. Mikey studied them suspiciously for several more moments.

"Okay." He finally relented as he looked at her. "But after we help Unca Ben, can I have a drink? I'm thirsty."

"Sure you can, sweetie." She patted his hand. "So, where's your uncle?"

"Down there." He walked a few steps before pointing downward.

Victoria had to peer through the gloom and whirling snow for several moments before she finally spotted the barely discernible fender of a white car that had clearly slipped off the road, down the embankment and into the forest. Its hood was crushed against a massive pine tree which also pinned the driver's door closed.

"Good man, Mikey." There was no signal on her phone. Frowning, Victoria spied a sheltered indentation in the rock face and led the boy there, figuring that since he was dressed warmly, he'd be okay for a bit. "You stay here, out of the wind. Don't try to follow me," she ordered firmly. "I'll go talk to Uncle Ben then come back."

Mikey frowned. "He's sleepin' an' he won't wake up."

Unconscious? Victoria's heart sank but praying was a habit she developed long ago. *Lord? Even after what I've done, are You still with me?*

"I'll check on him but you still have to stay here, Mikey."

"But what if a dinosaur comes? Or a crocodile?" he asked in a scared voice. "Or a bear?" He was so cute.

"Bears sleep in wintertime, honey. And crocodiles and dinosaurs don't live anywhere near these mountains," she promised. "Anyway, Spot and Dot won't let any animals get near you."

"Sure?" Mikey frowned when she nodded. "I don't like those biting dogs." He glared at them as he rubbed his arm.

"They didn't bite you, honey. They just grabbed on to your coat, to keep you safe. They're your friends, just like me. Understand?"

Mikey did not look convinced but finally, he nodded.

"I promise I'll hurry as fast as I can." After reassuring him again, Victoria slipped and slid her way down the embankment. Every so often, she called encouragements to Mikey and reminded him to stay put. She'd call for help as soon as she'd assessed the situation, after she checked on Uncle Ben. But she'd have to climb higher because there was no cell phone signal down here, either.

The car's rear passenger door hung open. Probably how Mikey escaped. After ensuring that the vehicle was firmly wedged and would not move, Victoria swept away the snow and peered inside. A very good-looking man, in a military haircut that emphasized his strong jaw, lay sprawled in the driver's seat with the airbag deployed around him. A bleeding gash marred his forehead, probably where he'd bashed into the cracked side window. He wore a dark fleece sweatshirt and jeans. His unzipped blue jacket looked new. She yanked open the front passenger door.

"Sir?" He didn't answer. Glad of the first-aid courses her employers had insisted she complete, Victoria quickly checked his vitals. All good. "Uncle Ben?"

He groaned, shifted slightly. Thick brown lashes lifted slowly until big blue eyes met hers.

"Hello." The slurred words were accompanied by a faint smile.

"I'm Victoria Archer. You went off the road. Do you remember?"

"No. Yes." He shook his head, winced and then whispered frantically, "Mikey! Where's Mikey?"

"He's safe. My dogs are guarding him."

"Mikey hates dogs." Ben licked his lips. "A year ago, one bit him."

"That explains it." At his questioning look, she shook her head. "Never mind. Other than the cut on your forehead, are you okay?"

"Lemme check." Ben closed his eyes as he completed a series of movements. Then he looked at her, his face grim as he listed his injuries. "Left arm's bruised but not broken. Ankle's wrenched. My ribs are probably going to bruise and my head hurts where I hit it. And my door's stuck."

"It's jammed against the tree. You'll have to get out on this side." She studied the situation. "Can you move?"

"Barely, but so what?" he asked gruffly. "You're too small to help me."

Too small. Fire sprang to life inside Victoria. She'd heard that all her life and she still hated it. As if her brainpower depended on her height.

"I'm strong, I'm smart and I *can* help you," she said, ignoring an inner flutter of appreciation for his blue eyes. "If *you* can get out."

"I've got a good sixty pounds on you," Ben grumbled, easing off his seat belt. "Even if I do get out, you can't support me, and I doubt I can walk, especially uphill."

"First let's see what we're dealing with," she said, reining in her temper. "Then I'll phone Jake, our hired hand, for help."

"Why not call a tow truck?" Ben clenched his jaw as he eased his body across the seat.

"Wouldn't do any good." Victoria tried to move his injured foot but knew from his sudden indrawn breath that it was less painful for him to do it himself. "In a storm like this, the Alberta Ministry of Transportation concentrates on ensuring the main roads in and out of Jasper and our nearest town, Chokecherry Hollow, are navigable. The Haven is always last on their plow-out list because we're the only ones who live along this road. Doesn't matter though because Jake usually has us plowed out long before they arrive. But that won't be for a while. It's coming down pretty heavily now."

"Huh." Ben was almost free when she suddenly realized there was no place except a snowbank for him to sit.

"Wait. Feeling okay?"

"Peachy," he shot back in a grumpy tone.

"Good." She grinned at his dour glance. "Stay here, on this passenger seat. Close the door to keep warm. Rest for a few minutes while I go call Jake and check on Mikey."

"Good idea." Ben grunted his assent, his

tanned face strained. "Kid's probably starving. It's a while since we ate."

"Not a problem." She closed the car door. So where did Uncle Ben get a tan like that, at this time of year, in Canada? He sure didn't get his tan from a bottle like Aunt Tillie did because Uncle Ben's skin was too evenly darkened, the deep color almost burned in. Maybe he was a skier?

Victoria told herself to forget her building questions about the guy as she climbed vertically, grasping twigs and rocks to help in her ascent. Mikey was where she'd left him, still glaring at the dogs.

"I found Uncle Ben," she said, puffing a little. "He's got a sore arm and leg. I need to phone someone to come help us."

"'Cause Unca Ben's really big," Mikey agreed, brown eyes huge.

"He sure is." She chuckled. "Are you warm enough?"

"Uh-huh. 'Fore we comed here, Unca Ben buyed me this coat and snow pants. They gots feathers in 'em."

"Like the birds, huh? Only you don't fly." Mikey looked confused by her silliness. "Good for Uncle Ben." She fished a granola bar out of her pocket and held it out. "Want to munch on this?" He nodded eagerly, took it and ripped off the paper. "Don't give any to the dogs," she warned and then almost laughed at his dubious expression. As if that was likely. "You stay here. I'm going to climb higher."

"Why?" Mikey asked, his mouth full.

"Because that's where my phone works. Don't move. I'll be back in a jiffy." Victoria's heart pinched when his lips trembled.

"It's gettin' dark," Mikey whispered. "I don't like dark. Bad things happen in dark."

What was that about?

"Good thing I brought my flashlight." Victoria showed the boy how to turn on her tiny pocket light and got his agreement to remain. Then she began her ascent.

Years of living in the Canadian Rockies and hours spent rock-wall climbing at a city gym meant Victoria had no difficulty scaling to the top. It took several moments to get a signal, but Jake was quick to answer and promised to help after he'd notified her family to prepare for guests.

"Bring the usual rescue gear," Victoria suggested. "Add a toboggan and some extra ropes, too. I doubt he can walk very far. We'll have to pull him up. I'll leave my scarf on a tree as a marker."

"He must be the guy your aunts expect," Jake said.

"Now that you mention it, I do remember hearing about a visitor arriving. But I didn't pay much attention." Because morning sickness was hitting her hard these days.

Assured Jake was coming, Victoria ended the call, attached her scarf to the bough of a needleless tamarack tree and then half slid, half climbed back down to Mikey. "Still warm enough?"

"Yeah. But I'm thirsty." He looked around. "Can I eat the snow?"

"No!" Realizing she'd scared him, Victoria made a funny face. But she had to ensure he wouldn't try it because eating snow would lower his body temperature. "This snow isn't clean, Mikey. My friend will bring you something warm to drink."

"Hot choc'lat?" he asked hopefully.

"Maybe." She crouched down to peer into his eyes. "Can you stay here a little longer while I check if Uncle Ben needs anything?"

Clearly thrilled by the promise of a drink, Mikey flicked on the flashlight and nodded. Victoria navigated down the cliff face again, grimacing at the protest in her calves.

"You're not as fit as you think, girl," she muttered in disgust.

"Yes, you are." Ben held the car door open. His blue eyes surveyed her with—admiration? "If I'd climbed up and down that steep slope as many times as you, my knees would be rubber."

"With your military training? I doubt it." Victoria smiled at the surprise filling his face and thrust out a hand. "Pleased to meet you. Major Adams, I presume?"

"You know me?" Ben asked. She liked his firm grip. Many men shook her hand as if they were holding a wet fish.

"The aunts mentioned that one of their military correspondents, a major, was coming to visit, but I doubt they expected you or Mikey during this storm." The roar of a snowmobile engine cut through the whine of wind. "That'll be Jake." She turned away. "I'll be back."

"Victoria?"

"Yes?" She glanced back at Ben.

"Is Mikey okay?" A tenderness lay behind the words. Ben got high marks from her for worrying about his nephew.

"He's got the dogs locked in a death stare. He ate a granola bar and he's thirsty. Other than that, he's doing fine." She took another step before adding, "You're fortunate this storm didn't arrive with some really frigid weather, Major."

Through the crackle of bushes and the approaching snowmobile, she thought she heard him mutter, "Fortunate? Me? Yeah, sure I am."

A sigh followed, making her wonder exactly what Ben meant.

* * *

"Dear Major, are you sure you're all right? Shouldn't you be in bed, resting?"

Though his arm throbbed something fierce, his midsection smarted and his ankle stung, Ben forced a smile at the elderly woman.

"I'm fine, Miss Spenser. Er, Tillie," he quickly corrected, using the name she'd requested. "I'm sorry to be a bother."

"We're delighted to have you and Mikey visit The Haven." Margaret Spenser was a doppelgänger for her twin sister in everything but demeanor. Where Tillie reminded Ben of a graceful Southern belle, Margaret bustled to fulfill some unspoken agenda. "God has certainly supplied your medical needs. Victoria's bandages look most effective."

"Yes, they are." He glanced from the sling holding his arm to his chest to the petite beauty sitting across from him. A straight fall of almost-black hair lovingly cupped Victoria's sculpted ivory face as she sat in a wingback chair with Mikey cuddled beside her. At the moment, she was studying him with her inscrutable gray eyes. Ben looked back at Margaret. "Thank you for your hospitality."

"You are more than welcome, dear. It's a good

thing you knew how to get our computer to scoop so Victoria could contact the doctor," Tillie said.

"Skype," he corrected, quickly realizing this lady neither knew nor cared about computers.

"Yes, it's called Skype, sister. Anyway, it's too bad we can't get you into Chokecherry Hollow, Ben. But at least Doc was able, with Victoria's help, to ascertain that your injuries aren't severe. Now, please excuse us while we go assist the other girls with dinner. Mikey, come and help us." Margaret lifted a hand when Victoria shifted as if to rise. "You stay here and entertain our guest, dear."

Ben didn't understand Victoria's frown nor the odd way she studied her aunts' retreating figures, Mikey between them. "Is something the matter?" he asked politely.

"I'm not sure." Victoria refocused on him. "But they have that look."

"What look?" Confused, Ben tried to recall something in the ladies' manner. "I didn't—"

"No, you wouldn't have." She gave him a strangled smile. "What brings you to The Haven, Ben?"

"Um," he blinked at the sudden switch in conversation. But there was no point in prevaricating. "I'm a peacekeeper with the United Nations in Central Africa. I became part of The Spenser sisters' campaign to write to soldiers when Tillie's first letter arrived about seven months ago. In every letter since, she invited me to The Haven. So I came. I'm hoping she can give me some advice. About Mikey."

"What kind of advice, if you don't mind me asking?" Victoria leaned forward in her chair, gray eyes widening with curiosity. She had the lush, long lashes his sister-in-law, Alice, had craved.

Alice and Neil. Gone. Ben's stomach clenched as grief billowed inside him. Only through sheer force of habit honed by peacekeeping could he maintain an implacable expression.

"Are you all right, Major?" Victoria had the kind of voice that revealed what she was thinking. Right now it said she knew he was hiding something and was offering to share his burden. For a moment, Ben was tempted.

But a second look made him doubt the elegant Victoria, with her stylish red turtleneck, chic red leather booties and probably designer jeans, had ever messed up her life. She wouldn't understand.

"Ben?" Worry now threaded her musical tone. "Doc Mendel said your pain might increase as the shock wears off. Do you have pain?"

Tons, but most isn't from wrecking the car.

He exhaled. *Get it said, man.*

"I'm on leave. I was visiting Mikey and his parents, my brother and sister-in-law. They were killed in a home invasion just over two months ago, while Mikey and I were at the zoo."

"Oh, no," Victoria gasped and immediately her almond-shaped eyes glossed with tears. "I'm so sorry. Poor you. Poor Mikey."

"Thanks. Anyway, now I'm his guardian and his godparent." Would she understand that he had to do the honorable thing for his nephew? "Before I return to my job overseas, I need to find Mikey a family he can live with, parents who will lovingly raise him. I have to make sure he's safe."

Silence yawned. Victoria stiffened. After a very long time, she whispered, "*You* can't raise him?"

Ben shook his head.

"Because?" She frowned, her wide, full lips tipping down in dismay.

"I'm nobody's idea of a parent, Victoria," he said when he could no longer remain silent. "I always fail at responsibility. Look at what happened today."

"That was an accident," she defended. "Not poor parenting."

"No, I should have waited a day. But I'm desperate to figure out a solution. I wanted to get here and talk to Tillie. I thought I could outrun the storm." Ben's lips tightened. "That's proof I'm not who Mikey needs."

"What does a—what is Mikey—four? What

does a four-year-old need?" She lifted her slim hand and ticked off her fingers. "Love, safety, security, a home. You can't give your nephew that?"

It was a question without innuendo, and yet Ben felt her condemnation to the depth of his soul. But doubts about his parenting ability weren't easy to purge.

"I don't think I can. Not properly. Taking care of Mikey is a matter of principle for me. Mikey comes first. Having a soldier for a parent is hardly what a young kid needs." Ben made a face. "And I do have to work."

"You can't find another way?" Victoria made a face. "Not that it's any of my business."

"It's okay," he sighed. "Believe me, I've tried. But I can't think of how."

"I see." She leaned back in her chair, her oval face disapproving. It was clear to Ben that she didn't see at all.

"I can't compromise about this, Victoria. Neil wouldn't want me to. He'd expect me to do my best for Mikey." A fierce protectiveness swelled inside. "I have to ensure that he's safe and cared for."

"Good." Was that relief on her face? Did she think he didn't care about his own nephew?

"Mikey's parents were committed to building their home and a happy family. I have neither to offer. Besides," he blurted, desperate to erase the fear growing inside, the worry that whatever he decided, he would make a mistake that would hurt his brother's precious son. "I'm not good with responsibility."

"Ben, you're a peacekeeper." Incredulity filled her voice.

"That's a job. I've been trained to follow orders but someone else makes the decisions. It isn't the same." Her face told him he needed to explain. "My mom was sick when I was a kid, Victoria. My dad, well, he wasn't around much so I was left to raise my brother. Neil was six years younger than me and we had opposite temperaments. I tried my best but—" It hurt to admit it aloud. "I didn't do right by him. I didn't know how. And because I failed him, he got into a lot of trouble."

"Neil blamed you?" Her dark eyebrows rose.

"No." Ben shook his head. "*I* blamed me. For not keeping him out of trouble. For not saving him from the whole gang-drug-jail trip. He finally broke free, no thanks to me, but in the end, his past and my failures caught up to him." How he hated saying this. "The police believe the people who murdered Alice and Neil were cronies from my brother's drug days, that they wanted money from him to score another hit."

"Oh, no." She looked as sad as he felt.

"Yeah. Neil started doing drugs because I demanded too much from him, so that makes his and Alice's deaths my fault." Ben almost gagged at the weight of that responsibility. "I might make the same mistake with Mikey and I can't risk that."

"You're not going to," Victoria shot back. "You're no longer some young, abandoned kid who's doing the best he can. You're an adult. Mikey started life with a stable family, parents who loved him. That's a whole different situation from Neil's. And now Mikey has you."

"No, he doesn't, because he can't depend on me." Ben glanced around the old-fashioned room as the knot inside him grew. "I'm not his father. I don't have the same knowledge, goals and experiences Neil would have passed on to Mikey. I have no idea how to be the kind of parent Mikey needs. I don't know anything about fatherhood."

"Fathers become fathers by learning." Victoria shrugged. "You can do the same."

"How? In furloughs? When I'm home for a couple months here and there? I can be sent anywhere at any time, into the worst hot spots. What if I was injured, or even killed?" He shook his head. "Mikey needs stable, full-time secure parents, here, in Canada."

Ben knew from the way Victoria's gray eyes turned to ice that she didn't agree. That's when he realized that Victoria, adamant in her principles, probably wasn't going to support his request to her aunts. Fortunately she didn't have a chance to voice the disapproval currently darkening her eyes because Tillie called them to the table.

With a sigh, Ben forced his focus off his rescuer and rose, gripping the handmade crutch Jake had made. He hobbled to the kitchen table, smothering a moan as his whole body protested. To his chagrin, Victoria's sisters and the two elderly ladies were already seated, leaving only two chairs unoccupied. When he sat beside Victoria, his arm brushed hers, creating a zip of electricity that made him even more tensely aware of her.

Everyone bowed their head as Margaret said grace. Once conversation flowed around them again Victoria leaned toward him.

"It won't make you less of a soldier to swallow a second painkiller, Major," she whispered. She poured him a glass of water then nodded at a small white pill sitting next to his knife.

Ben craved relief from the twinges that plagued him so he swallowed the tablet, hoping it wouldn't totally dull his senses because he had a hunch he was going to need his wits about him where this strong woman was concerned.

And yet, there was something else about Victoria—a vulnerability? Silly to say that about a woman who scaled mountains and rescued people. Yet Ben glimpsed a certain wistfulness in the tender brush of her hand against Mikey's head and the gentle way she teased him. Both belied a soft heart underneath the tough exterior she projected. He liked her pluck.

But Ben wasn't looking for a relationship. In fact, he never wanted to get involved, never wanted the obligation of caring for and probably failing a wife and family. He didn't want the responsibility of wrecking another young life. That's why he had to figure out Mikey's situation. His nephew's future was too precious to ruin, as he'd ruined Neil's.

As he ate, Ben struggled to stifle his growing interest in Victoria Archer. Maybe he didn't want to be, but he *was* very interested in this competent woman and why she'd been so insistent that Ben be Mikey's father.

He also wondered how long she'd be staying here, at The Haven, in the middle of nowhere. She was young, obviously hip and unmarried, judging by her bare ring finger. Her affection for the elderly sisters was obvious, her manner with them protective.

Though she seemed at home here at The Haven, Ben didn't get the feeling that Victoria lived here full-time. Or hadn't until recently. Comments from her sisters and her aunts about finally coming home made him want to know more about her.

When Mikey burst out bawling because the

apple crisp dessert reminded him of his mom, Victoria didn't try to change the subject or avoid the topic. Instead she wrapped a comforting arm around his shoulders and encouraged more memories. Within minutes, she had his nephew giggling as she tried to demonstrate his description of butterfly kisses.

Suddenly Ben hoped it would take Tillie and Margaret a while to find Mikey a family, long enough for him to figure out what made Victoria's gray eyes turn to soot when she didn't think anyone was watching.

Chapter Two

"Oh. You're still up."

Victoria paused in the doorway of the biggest room at The Haven, which was also the only one with a lit fireplace. Tillie and Margaret called this room The Salon but she'd always known it as their family room, the place where they'd shared their lives. Now it was occupied by their visitor.

"Couldn't sleep. Probably because I ate too much of your sister's delicious chicken pie." Firelight flickered across Ben, seated in Margaret's wingback chair in front of the fire, with Tillie's lurid purple-and-green afghan covering his legs. "What's that?"

"Hot chocolate. Want some?" Victoria didn't want to share with him. In fact, she wished he'd stayed in his room. She wanted to be alone, to think things through, to figure out her next step.

But she couldn't think with Ben nearby because his searching blue eyes made her nervous, fidgety.

Still, he was a guest and the aunts' lessons on hospitality had been deeply engrained in her.

"I'll get another cup."

"Don't bother," he called as Victoria scurried away like the frightened mouse she felt but didn't want anyone to see.

She drew a deep breath for control, patted her unsettled stomach, wondering if morning sickness could also be evening sickness and if its cause now was that her baby knew his mother didn't have a job now, or even a next step planned. Grimacing, she grabbed another mug and returned.

"No bother. There's more in that carafe than I can drink anyway." She filled his mug and set it on the round table, near his elbow. She added another log to the fire before sinking into Tillie's chair and cuddling her own cup while her brain scrambled for a topic of conversation. Ben beat her to it.

"Are there a lot of fireplaces in this house?" His gaze slid from the river-stone chimney to the massive fir mantel and granite-slab hearth.

"Yes. The Haven was built to be self-sufficient. Thankfully there's enough deadwood on the property to fuel the fireplaces." She loved this sagging, worn chair, not for the comfort it offered but for the memories it evoked. "Tom and Jerry were very smart men."

"Tom and Jerry being?" Ben studied her, one eyebrow arched in an inquisitive expression.

"How long has Aunt Tillie been writing you?" Victoria couldn't believe he hadn't heard the whole story already.

"Just over seven months. Why?"

"My aunts started writing letters to military personnel more than twenty years ago when they joined the local Legion. A former colonel suggested those who protect and serve our country might need someone to talk to and since the aunts missed their missionary work, they wrote." Victoria smiled at the memories of all the service men and women who'd visited The Haven during her teen years. Could she give her child such good memories?

"That's a lot of letters," Ben murmured.

"After a couple of years, the aunts developed a format. They usually give some personal history within the first two or three letters. Did they do that with you?" When he shook his head, she inhaled before explaining. "So how did you make contact with Aunt Tillie?"

"She wrote to me, said she was praying for Africa and my name was on the list of servicemen serving there. She asked if I had any special requests. Some of my buddies said I should write back." Ben smiled. "Tillie was the one who led me to God. So what's the history of The Haven?"

"That's a long story. It starts with brothers, Tom and Jerry *Haven*ston, hence The Haven. Tillie and Margaret were nurses and met the two when they were visiting Chokecherry Hollow. The aunts fell in love with the brothers. The four wanted to be married, but the ladies had already promised to go as missionaries to what was then Rhodesia."

"So I guess the brothers planned to go, too?" Ben asked.

"Yes, but Jerry contracted scarlet fever. Tillie and Margaret delayed their departure to nurse him at a friend's home but his recovery was very slow." As usual, Victoria felt a rush of sympathy for the two couples.

"I'm listening," Ben encouraged.

"The missions' society sponsoring the aunts kept pressing them to leave to replace other missionaries due to return to Canada. Jerry and Tom did, too. They wanted the sisters to keep their commitment to the society."

"Why?" Ben frowned.

"Because as the sons of missionaries who'd served in Africa, Tom and Jerry knew what the mission meant to the Africans. They insisted the aunts shouldn't break their promise to the society," Victoria explained.

"Strong men." Ben sounded approving.

"Very. Anyway, Tillie and Margaret left believing their fiancés would join them later. They were in Africa four months before they learned Tom had had a heart attack rendering him unable to travel. The aunts prepared to return, but the men telegrammed begging them to stay. The men had heard rumors that if left understaffed, the government would probably close the sisters' Rhodesian mission. They did not want Tillie and Margaret to alter what they believed was God's will."

"So they stayed here and built The Haven," Ben guessed.

"You're jumping way ahead," Victoria protested.

"Missionaries get furloughs, don't they?" Ben asked.

"Yes. A month after Tillie and Margaret returned to Canada, Tom had a second heart attack. And another after that. Everyone feared he'd die." Victoria could hardly bear to think of her aunts' distress. "Aunt Tillie told me she and Margaret took turns nursing him until he slowly recovered. The aunts returned to Rhodesia after Tom and Jerry agreed they'd follow when possible. Again they made plans to marry."

"Even fifty years ago, it must have taken a fortune to buy all the land and build The Haven." Ben frowned. "The aunts gave up a comfy life."

"Oh, the brothers weren't wealthy at first. In fact, they supported their widowed and ailing sister and her two children." Victoria smiled. "It took years before they became successful. But I digress."

"They couldn't go to Africa," Ben guessed.

"No, because their sister died, leaving them guardians of her daughters. Both were sickly. Tom and Jerry eventually realized that their own poor health would never allow them to travel to Africa." Victoria saw empathy flash across his face.

"Just shows how our plans can change in an instant," he murmured.

Boy, did Victoria know about that. She'd never planned to be a single mother.

"Go on." Ben leaned forward in his eagerness to hear the story. She liked that he was so interested in the aunts' history.

"Well, after much prayer, the men decided God had planned a different future for them. They raised their nieces in the fresh mountain air, which seemed to help their unhealthy lungs," she said.

"And then?"

"Tom and Jerry invented a medical item that helped hospitals enormously and made them wealthy. They bought acres of land and built this house, a home for their nieces and for Tillie and

Margaret when they finally returned to Canada for good." She waved a hand. "Tom and Jerry lovingly thought out every detail of The Haven. They were amazing men who truly loved the aunts."

"But Tillie's always signed her letters *Miss*." Ben's blue-eyed gaze studied her. "Didn't they marry after all?"

"I have to tell it in sequence, Ben," Victoria chided. "The nieces contracted polio and never recovered, dying just weeks before the aunts finally returned here. After a period of mourning, the four again planned their long-anticipated weddings." Victoria paused in the sad tale, then added, "Tom and Jerry went on a bachelor hiking trip through their beloved mountains three days before the weddings. They were fatally shot by illegal poachers."

"Oh, no. After all that waiting." She liked that Ben seemed genuinely moved. Proved he was nothing like stone-cold Derek who felt nothing for his own child. "It must have been hard to accept that, after all their sacrifice, God didn't give the sisters their own happy ending."

"Didn't He?" Victoria tried not to smile, relieved Tillie and Margaret hadn't heard that. "Tom and Jerry left their fortunes and The Haven to the sisters to, as they put it, continue their missionary work. So the aunts got busy being missionaries in their community."

She stretched her neck, suddenly weary. This motherhood thing was taxing.

"That wasn't enough," Ben guessed.

"The colonel I mentioned earlier? He knew someone who agreed to provide them with the names of troops they could write to. And thus began the sisters' letter-writing ministry."

"Amazing story. Bad turned to blessings." Ben nodded. "A lot of men in my unit really look forward to the ladies' letters, you know. I'm one of them. I've also heard how they often have veterans visiting here."

"They often do, but there's a lot more to my aunties than that." Victoria grinned.

"Meaning?"

Of course she wouldn't tell Ben the whole truth about herself, but she did want him to realize how important Tillie and Margaret were in so many lives.

"You met my sisters Adele and Olivia at dinner tonight though I doubt much sunk in. You were hurting pretty badly."

"I'm sorry I had such poor manners," Ben said, looking embarrassed.

"They understood. They're used to hurting people showing up here. All of us are. We were some of them once." She chuckled at his confused look. "Let me explain. When I was ten and my sisters a bit younger—by the way, we have a fourth foster sister, Gemma. Anyway, we four girls were troublemakers headed down a bad road. We all had the same caseworker and she wanted us away from the gang we were about to join. So she asked the aunts to fund trips to camp for all four of us."

"You liked it there?" Ben asked.

"We four girls had never met before but being bad apples, we banded together and caused no end of problems in that camp." How she regretted that.

"I find it hard to believe you were a troublemaker, Victoria." He frowned.

"Believe it. The camp wanted us gone. In desperation, our caseworker contacted her friends Tillie and Margaret again and, ignoring their ages, asked them to take all four of us for three months. No one else would touch us for a week, so asking for three months was asking a lot."

"You're kidding." Ben's gaping stare made her smile.

"Not at all. We were all experienced foster brats. We'd all learned how to fool everyone. Except once we got to The Haven, we couldn't fool Tillie and Margaret." She chuckled at the memory of their pranks. "Short story—we four girls grew up here with abundant love demonstrated every day. The service men and women the aunts host here made a big impact on us. So did the aunts' offers to accommodate countless local programs for various charity groups. We grew up seeing missionaries in action."

"So Tom and Jerry's Haven has truly become a haven for a lot of people." Ben's blue eyes stretched wide. "Quite a story."

"It is." Victoria sipped her cocoa thoughtfully. "But I don't know how much longer that can continue."

"What do you mean?" Ben's forehead furrowed. "Are Tillie and Margaret broke?"

"Oh, no. Tom and Jerry invested very wisely." Victoria exhaled. "It's more to do with aging. We four girls moved out, pursued careers, got on with our lives. But the aunts are still here, much older and virtually alone, except for Jake, and he can't run the place alone forever, though he'd argue otherwise."

"So Tillie and Margaret have to leave The Haven?" Ben asked quietly.

"Not without a struggle." Victoria grimaced. "Since I'm home for a while, I'm hoping to figure out a way for them to stay a little longer. If Aunt Maggie hasn't already beaten me to it," she added darkly.

"What does that mean?"

Victoria bit her lip.

"You don't want to tell me?" he prodded.

"It's not that. It's—my aunts get a lot of ideas."

Sitting here in the twilight, talking with Ben—it wasn't as bad as Victoria had expected. In fact, maybe he'd have some thoughts on how to keep the aunts in their home. "Some of their ideas are, well, let's call them outlandish."

"I see." Ben's intense stare made her nervous. And yet it was also somehow comforting to talk out her fears. She certainly couldn't have done it with Derek. At least Ben didn't try to make her feel silly or stupid.

"The thing is, even their most bizarre ideas often work. Eventually," she mumbled, wishing her usual proficiency with fixing things hadn't suddenly deserted her.

"You think your aunts have a plan for how they can stay here?" Ben asked.

"Something Aunt Margaret said before she went to bed makes me think the two of them have come up with a new scheme." Victoria read his face and chuckled. "You think that's good. It might be. It might also turn out to be totally, utterly impossible. In which case," she explained, leaning forward so he'd understand, "my sisters and I will have to gently disabuse them of the notion."

"Having met the two ladies, I'm guessing that won't be easy." Ben tried and failed to smother his amusement. Suddenly he sat up straight. "Was that Mikey calling? Since we, er, found his parents' bodies, he's had nightmares and—"

"Being afraid is probably normal for all little kids sometimes. But I have a monitor in Mikey's room, Ben." She pulled it out of her pocket. "Listen." She held it up. All that transmitted was the sound of smooth, even breathing. "He's fine, but I can go check on him if that will make you feel better."

"Do you mind?" He glanced at his foot. "I'd do it but that spiral staircase is daunting."

"I take it you're happy with your main-floor room down the hall, then?" She chuckled at his forceful nod and rose. "Back in a jiffy."

Snugging her ancient and tattered velvet robe around her waist, Victoria scooted up the stairs. Mikey was fast asleep just like her aunts who were snoring. There were no sounds from the room Olivia shared with Adele so Victoria padded down the stairs in her fluffy slippers and reentered the salon.

"Everything's good, Ben." She scanned his tense face. "But I don't think you are."

"It's my leg. I need to elevate it. I'd better get to bed." He rose slowly, using his crutch. "Thanks for checking on Mikey and the cocoa and the talk, Victoria. I'll pray about The Haven's future though I'm not sure it will do much good. I'm pretty new at the whole praying thing."

"New Christian or old, doesn't make a difference to God. 'The Lord has set apart the redeemed for Himself. Therefore He will listen to me and answer when I call upon Him,'" she quoted. "That's what David said in the fourth chapter of Psalms."

"That's a verse I need to memorize," he murmured thoughtfully. "So often I feel like God doesn't hear me, especially when I see the heartache and devastation in my job. To know that God always listens—that's comforting." He stared directly into her eyes. "I'm impressed that you can quote the Bible so easily."

"Part and parcel of living with Tillie and Margaret." Victoria smiled. "The Bible is an intricate part of their lives and, by association, those around them." *And you've failed to live up to their and your own Biblical principles.* A chill ran up her spine. Soon she'd be telling him all of it— "Good night, Ben."

"Good night." He continued to study her for several moments. Then he awkwardly wheeled around and thumped across the oak floor, toward his room down the hall.

Victoria waited until she heard his door close before resuming her seat in the armchair, her brain whirling with questions.

How was she going to help the aunts stay at The Haven?

How was she going to raise a baby on her own, with no visible means of support? How was she going to stand seeing the disappointed looks on her aunts' faces when she told them? She'd already caused them so much heartache when she first came here. Maybe they wouldn't even want her anymore.

Just how much could their love endure?

Her fingers splayed over her midsection.

God, are You mad at me?

She'd just assured Ben that God always listened, but deep inside her heart, Victoria felt a void, an emptiness she'd never known before. She knew why that was. She'd disregarded the principles she'd been raised on. Maybe God was now leaving it up to her to handle having and raising this baby alone. She was no weakling, but being strong enough for that scared Victoria to her core.

The next morning, Ben savored the delicious breakfast Adele had prepared.

"Olivia and I have to get back to work," she'd explained as she shrugged into her coat. "Since Jake plowed out the road last night to take you into the doctor this morning, we'll get an early start. Olivia has to catch a flight to Ottawa. She works there for the military. I live in Edmonton and I have a catering job scheduled for tomorrow so I have to go, too."

"Have a good trip," he said with a smile.

"Thanks. Vic's still sleeping. I left a note telling her we'll text later."

"I hope we see you and Mikey again, Ben," Olivia added.

"Me, too," he said, and meant it.

After hugging their aunts and promising to return soon, the two left. Then Jake appeared and said he'd be driving Ben to town. Conscious of his lack of mobility and wearied by the physical strain of getting in and out of the doctor's office, Ben was glad to return to The Haven.

"The doctor said you'll be fine?" Margaret nodded when he repeated the diagnosis of rest. "Good. You and Mikey can stay and relax."

"Thank you. And thank you for watching him while I went into town." He sipped his coffee, glad the boy had slept in until a few minutes ago.

"I wish the girls could have stayed a little longer." Tillie cuddled her coffee mug in her hand. "It's so much fun when they're here."

"Maybe, with the right incentive, they'll come back." Margaret wore a quirky smile that Ben thought was somewhat cunning.

"What's the right incentive, Auntie?" Victoria stumbled into the kitchen, trying to smother a gigantic yawn and failing. Ben thought she looked awful.

"My dear, are you ill?" Tillie rushed to Victoria's side and ushered her to a chair at the table. "Your face is positively gray!"

"I slept in too long. Maybe that's why I feel a little off this morning," Victoria admitted.

A little off? Not the way Ben would have put it.

"Coffee might help," Margaret suggested.

Perhaps he was the only one who saw Victoria almost gag.

"I'll wait a bit, thanks, Auntie."

"I'm sorry if rescuing us caused you to be ill," he apologized.

"It didn't." Victoria avoided looking at him. As if to divert attention from herself, she asked Mikey if he'd slept well.

"I had a good sleep," his nephew said with a grin. "When I waked up, I saw your little light."

"Auntie Margaret gave me that light after I came here to live." Victoria smiled at her aunt. "I was older than you are, Mikey, but I still had bad dreams. Auntie said that when I woke up afraid, I should look at the lamp and remember that Jesus was right beside me, protecting me."

"Like you said to me!" Mikey exclaimed. "I did an' it worked. I didn't get 'fraid."

"I'm glad. Excuse me." Victoria suddenly burst from her chair and bolted from the room.

"Oh, the poor dear." Tillie put on the kettle. "I'll make her some peppermint tea."

"I'll get some crackers." Margaret frowned as

she set the packet on the table. "The child is so thin. It's not healthy."

"It's the fashion now and she's hardly a child." Tillie smiled as Victoria returned, looking, in Ben's opinion, even more pasty-faced than before. "All right, dear?"

"Just a flu bug." She studied his sling. "That doesn't look like my work."

"This morning, Jake drove me in to see the doctor who checked it then redid it. He said your work was very professional." Ben couldn't help wondering if Victoria actually heard him. She looked as if she was thinking about something else.

"That's nice." She smiled wanly before tearing open the crackers. "Too bad the girls had to leave."

"Yes, it is." Tillie exchanged what Ben thought was an odd look with her sister.

"We never had a chance to tell them our idea," Margaret murmured.

"Your—idea?" Victoria suddenly went still. She glanced from one senior to the other before asking in a hesitant voice, "What's your idea, Aunties?"

"To make The Haven a—a spa. Is that the word, sister?" Tillie looked to Margaret for clarification.

Ben watched Victoria's eyes widen. She seemed to scramble for a response.

"A spa is a—good idea, Aunties," she managed to say. "The Haven has a wonderful location. But—well, we don't have any pools or hot tubs or mud baths or masseuses. You know," she continued when the aunts looked confused, "the usual spa things that draw people."

"Oh, no, dear. Spa's the wrong word." Tillie frowned at Margaret. "Can you explain?"

"Think retreat," Margaret clarified. "A retreat for kids. Troubled kids. Foster kids. Like you were, Victoria."

Ben immediately saw the potential. Acres of land for hikes to wear kids out. Wild animals to observe, room to relax and allow nature's peace to calm tortured hearts.

"For kids?" Victoria frowned. "But there's nothing here for kids!"

"There was for you," Margaret reminded tartly.

"Yes, but that was years ago, Auntie. Today's kids are techies, constantly connected. They'd need organized activities—" She stopped, no doubt aware of the sisters' growing irritation.

"I can see it." Ben probably should have shut up given Victoria's annoyed glance in his direction. But he couldn't. "Trails to hike, endurance or training courses, a chance to work with the cows and chickens you have. Kids might really enjoy a place like this."

"You know a lot about kids?" Victoria demanded, probably reminding him of his claim not to know how to parent. But Ben let his imagination go.

"I don't, but I'd guess the river I've seen crossing the valley could offer decent swimming in the summer," he mused.

"Where would these kids stay?" Victoria's question was directed at her aunts. "They have to sleep somewhere. They'd need counsellors or someone to watch them." She scowled. "There are only ten bedrooms here in The Haven."

"There are the cabins," Margaret replied.

Ben glanced through the big window but saw no buildings.

"Aunties, the cabins haven't been used in years. They're decrepit and..." Victoria's tone bordered on exasperation.

"No, they're not." Tillie's normally soft voice was loud and firm. "Jake checked them over for us. He did some repairs himself and oversaw local volunteers who helped with others. Bottom line, we have eight cabins that will each sleep four, five at a pinch. Maggie's already ordered new mattresses for the cots," she added defiantly.

"We weren't going to say that, Tillie," her sister admonished. "But since you have..." She shrugged. "We also ordered some canoes. Boating on the river was something our boys enjoyed so much," she explained to Ben.

Boys? he wondered.

"Our fiancés were real outdoorsmen," Tillie agreed with a reminiscent smile.

Victoria looked dumbfounded. Mikey glanced curiously from one woman to the other. Ben was intrigued.

"Describe who you envision coming here," he murmured.

"Children like our four girls," Tillie said with a smile at Victoria. "Kids who need to escape the lure of drugs or whatever evil they're trapped in. Or perhaps they and their foster families simply need a break from each other, time to think."

"We're still in touch with the foster system in Edmonton, you know," Margaret added with a pointed look at her foster daughter. "They think it's a wonderful idea."

"I'm sure they do." Victoria chewed another cracker.

"You think we're too old, don't you?" Tillie frowned. "Well, we'll never be too old to answer when the Lord calls us."

"Are you sure *He* called you, Auntie?" Victoria's normally musical voice had a frosty edge. "Or was it your friends in Social Services who made you think this was a good idea?"

Ben watched the twins draw erect, their annoyance obvious.

"We have thought and prayed about this decision for months, Victoria. We've conducted many inquiries into how the logistics would work, the cost, the need for helpers," Margaret spoke clearly, her voice confident. "We have sought the Lord over and over to ascertain His will. We believe this is it."

"You're going ahead with it." The words carried resignation.

"We'd like to." Tillie took her hand. "On one condition."

"We've been praying that you'd be willing to help us," Margaret finished.

"Me?" Victoria's dark head reared back, gray eyes wide. "How could I help?"

"My dear, you are a fixer, a problem-solver for the hotel. You didn't train for it. You trained to be a teacher. But when your school closed, you took the hotel job and mastered anticipating and resolving situations that frustrated others. You made things work. That's what we want, someone who will enable our idea. Right, Maggie?" She looked to Margaret who nodded once.

"But—but—" Victoria's glance moved around the table, staring at each one of them. Ben felt her gaze rested on him longest.

"May I ask something?" he said quickly, desperate to know if his trip had been in vain.

"Please do." Tillie inclined her head.

"Does your new plan mean you'll stop writing people in the military? That you won't want them to come to The Haven anymore?"

"We see the two meshing. Veterans who visit The Haven may be willing to interact with our guests, even become mentors." Margaret's words came crisp and clear. "We think they'd have much to offer."

"And that brings us to the reason you came to see us, doesn't it?" Tillie's smile warmed him, chased away the fear that had hatched inside him. "Let's go to the study and talk about your situation, Ben. I'm sure Victoria and Mikey can find something to do until we're finished." She rose, linked her arm with her sister's and beckoned him before they walked out.

"Coming." Ben rose and moved awkwardly toward the door. He paused by Victoria, touched by the confusion in her eyes. "Their plan upset you. Will you be all right?"

"Eventually." Her smile held more determination than mirth. "Go. Mikey and I will be fine." She grimaced and jumped up. "Right after I'm sick." She scurried from the room as if chased.

"Is Vic okay, Unca Ben?" Mikey sounded worried he'd lose another adult from his world.

Ben couldn't respond because he'd time-traveled back to Neil's, sitting in the kitchen, watching as his sister-in-law, Alice, turned green and then raced away.

"Is she okay?" he'd asked his brother.

"Alice is fine. Just pregnant."

Could Victoria be pregnant?

Brain whirling, Ben ordered Mikey to stay put and hobbled out of the kitchen to answer Tillie's impatient call.

Was Victoria going to be a mom? A mental picture of her cradling a tiny baby in her arms stuck with Ben all through his conversation with the elderly sisters.

Why was he so certain Victoria would be an amazing mother? It was obvious. She was kind and generous and obviously willing to put her own wants after the needs of her elderly aunts. And she was great with Mikey.

But where was the baby's father? Did she love him? Was she planning to marry soon? And why did that thought bug him?

Ben had a hunch that Victoria was keeping the news from her aunts and probably her sisters also since none of them had offered congratulations. But why?

All of these questions and hundreds more made Ben decide to question Victoria. Maybe she'd explain it as she'd explained about her aunts. He felt this intense need to know everything about her, though in truth, it wasn't any of his business.

Chapter Three

With her stomach upset, her mind troubled by the aunts' grandiose plans for The Haven and her heart even more bothered that Ben was considering letting Mikey be adopted, Victoria couldn't sit still, so she did what she always did when she needed to think. She went for a long walk through the forest—with Mikey.

"What're those marks in the snow?" he wanted to know.

"Rabbit tracks." *Kids, here at The Haven?*

"What's that big block?"

"Salt. Deer like to lick it." *Why not kids at The Haven? As Auntie said, we four sisters found plenty to do here.*

"Why is that tree black?"

"Forest fire." Victoria smiled at his worried look. "We don't have forest fires in the winter, Mikey, and even if we did, there's a lot more equipment to fight them now than there was when this one happened."

Safety—another reason why inviting kids out to the mountains wasn't a great idea. They could get lost or injured.

"I wish I could live here." Mikey's comment jerked her out of her thoughts.

"You do?" Victoria hid a smile as he veered away from the panting dogs. "Even though Spot and Dot live at The Haven?" Mikey's emphatic nod said a lot. "How come?"

"There's no bad men here," he whispered. "They won't get me an' Unca Ben."

"No, they sure won't," Victoria assured him.

But that was hardly comfort enough. She tried to imagine what she would tell her own child in such a situation. For sure she'd want to soothe him. Maybe she'd gather him on her knee, hug him close and tell him the Bible story of how God protected little Samuel, just as her foster aunts had told her.

As Mikey's anxious face searched hers for answers, Victoria knew she couldn't fail him so she crouched beside him and drew him into the circle of her arms.

"Nobody's going to get you, sweetheart," she comforted, moved by his little-boy-lost expression. "Uncle Ben's nearby. And God's looking after you."

"He didn't look after my mommy an' daddy." Clearly Mikey was troubled.

Victoria wasn't sure how to respond, but she didn't have to because he added in a very quiet voice, "Me an' Unca Ben woulda been there to 'tect Mommy and Daddy if I didn't ask for ice cream."

"Oh, no, my darling." Victoria's heart ached for the blame he carried. Mikey and Ben both felt responsible for something over which they had no control. "Listen to me, Mikey. Having ice cream with your uncle didn't make those men hurt your parents. You are not to blame."

"But Unca Ben coulda stopped them if we'd gone home. He coulda," he assured her with a frown. "Unca Ben is big and strong. His job is to 'tect people."

"I know." Victoria bit her lip. She could hardly reassure Mikey that his uncle would be here to protect him because that wasn't true. Ben felt he had to find someone else to do that—unless she, or perhaps the aunts, could change his mind. "Mikey, God's even bigger than Uncle Ben. He can keep you safe when Uncle Ben's not there. You can trust God. When you're afraid, you can pray and ask Him to make the fear go away. God's your Heavenly Father and He loves you very much."

After studying her silently, Mikey resumed

plodding through the snow. Victoria inwardly winced at his sad expression, glad for the silence as recrimination filled her. How dare she tell others to trust—she who hadn't trusted God to find her a man deserving of her love? She'd failed to live up to standards her aunts had ingrained in her. What kind of example would she be to kids who came to The Haven? How could a pregnant single woman talk to them about God, about keeping His commandments? Her cheeks burned with shame.

She kept glancing at Mikey as they walked. Why couldn't Ben see that Mikey needed him? Now more than ever. She sighed with frustration. Walking had failed to provide her with the answers she craved.

When they returned to the house, Ben waited for them in the kitchen.

"Are you all right?" His dark blue eyes inspected her face.

"I'm fine." She turned away to make some toast. "The fresh air up here always does wonders for me."

"Uh-huh." Something in the way he said that made her twist to look at him. Disliking the speculative look on his face, she quickly changed the subject. "Mikey saw lots of interesting things."

Thankfully that sent the boy into a long-winded explanation of the sights and sounds around The

Haven, leaving Victoria, who was suddenly ravenous, to munch on toast and peanut butter between sips of well-creamed coffee.

"What do you have planned today?" Ben asked when she finally rose to put her dishes in the dishwasher.

"Well, since Olivia and Adele are gone, I suppose lunch will be up to me. Unless—" She checked the fridge and then pumped her fist. "Yes! My dear sister left us a huge pot of soup which means I don't have to cook."

"I can cook if you need help," Ben offered.

"That's nice of you, though I *can* cook. Tillie and Margaret would never have allowed us girls to leave The Haven without knowing how to care for ourselves." She wrinkled her nose as she set a coloring book and crayons in front of Mikey. "It's just that cooking's not my favorite activity."

"What is?" Ben accepted a refill of coffee before leaning back in his chair and waiting.

"Almost any kind of sport. Or anything to do with kids or animals." She glanced from him to Mikey before asking, "Were you able to discuss—things, while we were walking?"

"Yes." He studied his nephew with a frown. "The ladies are writing a few letters. This afternoon they're going to town to mail them and—er—check into some possibilities."

"Ben, are you sure about this?"

"Pretty sure." His mouth tightened in a grim line. "I can't think of any other way."

Victoria studied Mikey. "It's just—"

"What do you think of Tillie and Margaret's idea for The Haven's newest outreach?" Now *he* was trying to change the subject.

"Over the top." Victoria grimaced. "But that's par for the course for them."

"I think it's amazing." Ben's face blazed with interest. "Think of the possibilities. What kid wouldn't want to come here?"

"If only it were that easy," she muttered.

"You mean your aunts don't have the qualifications or certifications or whatever they need?"

"I'm pretty sure they do. Tillie and Margaret took all the necessary courses to foster long before they brought us here. And they're diligent about keeping up with the foster system, constantly adding to their knowledge." She tapped her finger against her mug. "But more importantly, they have good contacts."

"In Jasper, you mean?" Ben looked confused.

"Jasper, Edmonton, Vancouver, Toronto. You name the place and I can almost guarantee my aunts know someone there who knows someone who knows someone." Victoria grinned at his visible skepticism. "It's true. How do you think they got to know so many people?"

"Tell me." His shrug made her chuckle.

"Their colonel, of course." Victoria shrugged back at him. "When vets the aunts had written to came for a visit here at The Haven, they told the ladies about the appalling situations they and some of their buddy veterans now lived in. Of course, the aunties had to do something. They enlisted the colonel and his colonel and general buddies to petition the government to spend more on those who'd given their service to this country. Because of the huge support, government response was enacted."

"Good for them," Ben said.

"Yes, but more importantly, as folks learned of Tillie and Margaret's original letter-writing, they began asking the aunts to write to their deployed family members. My dear aunties' letter-writing ministry grew." She smiled. "They always include a word about God and invite everyone to visit. Many come to thank them or seek their advice. My aunties have led a lot of people to Jesus and thus continues their missionary work," she said proudly.

"Now they want to extend it to foster kids. Judging by their past success, I'd say their idea has a good chance of success," he mused quietly.

"Of course it does," Victoria said crisply.

"But you don't want it to?" The words had barely left Ben's lips when he recanted. "No, that's not right. You love these ladies. Naturally you want them to succeed. So what's your stumbling block?" He watched her closely.

"The amount of work. They can take a rest from letter-writing if they need to, but running this place as a retreat will be nonstop. They're seventy-five, Ben."

"They seem younger."

"They can't run the kind of place they're describing alone. They'll need employees, payroll, insurance, programs, knowledge of regulations and, I'm sure, renovations," Victoria sighed. "There will be a ton of stuff involved."

"You don't want to help? Because you're afraid of the work or…? Say, what do you do again?" he asked suddenly.

"I am—was, a fixer for a hotel chain."

"A—huh?" Ben's confusion made her smile.

"A fixer. Solver of problems. If hotel rooms are empty too often, I figure out why and devise strategies so they'll be booked. If a hotel restaurant isn't working to capacity, they send me to figure it out. If clients are complaining about something too frequently, or we're not getting enough repeat business—actually any problems the hotel couldn't solve on its own were my problem. My job was to fix them. And I did."

"Sounds interesting and challenging." Ben's blue eyes stretched wide.

"It was. But it meant a lot of traveling, and I'm

tired of that. I'm a Big Sister to several preteen girls in Edmonton whom I dearly love. So much travel made it difficult to interact with them as much as they need." She grimaced. "I guess I haven't made things better by coming here either, though I tried to explain."

"How do you train for a job like that?" Curiosity filled Ben's question.

"I didn't. I trained as a teacher. I loved it, but my salary couldn't cover all the things I wanted to do with my Little Sisters, so I started as a part-time host on the hotel's main desk." She shrugged. "Stuff came up and I handled it. Then my school closed and I was laid off. I couldn't get on anywhere else. The hotel manager offered me full-time hours." *No need to tell Ben about Derek.* "After the first year, head office noticed our hotel didn't have the volume of complaints others in the chain did. Somebody decided I was the reason and things kind of took off from there."

"Good for you." Ben's stare seemed riveted on her.

"Thanks. I loved my job, but I need a break, so I've taken a leave." She shifted uncomfortably, answering Mikey's question about the right color to use for the stone house he was drawing while trying to think of a way to ignore questions she knew Ben would ask.

"You could do the same sort of thing here, with

your aunts' ideas," he mused. "But you want to go back to the city."

"No." Victoria's emphatic denial startled him. "I'm happy to bend over backward if the aunts ask me to. I just don't want *them* doing it." She could see he still didn't get it. "They should be retired, enjoying life."

"They're not enjoying life now?" He chuckled. "Could have fooled me. I've only been here a day but it looks as if those two ladies are having the times of their lives."

"I mean I want them to slow down, not take on even more. They've already got their fingers in so many pies." She ticked them off on her fingers. "Missionary society, teaching quilting to high school girls, programs at the seniors' center, not to mention their letter-writing and tons of stuff at their church." She bit her lip before lowering her voice. "Tillie and Margaret are my family, Ben. I don't want them worn out or tired. Inviting kids, keeping them busy, handling the seesaw of teen emotions and staff issues—I don't want them upset by that."

"Because you love them." Ben nodded in empathy. "And maybe you're afraid of losing them?"

Victoria jerked her head up to glare at him. Then she wearily nodded. It was an unspoken truth she'd never dared voice.

"I get all that, believe me. You're a good daughter and you want the best for them." Ben held her gaze. "But Tilly and Margaret aren't the type to be content sitting in their chairs, watching television or playing cards. You must know that, Victoria."

"Yes." Slightly annoyed that he was so perceptive, she was also relieved to have her thoughts challenged. "I guess it's a good thing I'm here."

"Part of God's plan," he agreed with a grin.

Single mom—*God's* plan? Victoria gulped. *If Ben only knew.*

"I don't think God had much to do with my coming back to The Haven," she muttered, feeling her face burn with shame. "Excuse me. I need to change before I make lunch."

"But you said the soup—"

Victoria ignored him, scurried out of the kitchen and up the stairs as if dogs were on her heels. In the privacy of her room, she collapsed on the bed and gazed at the molded plaster ceiling.

Part of God's plan, Ben said. As if God would be part of the mess she'd made of her life.

May the Lord bless and protect you; may the Lord's face radiate with joy because of you; may He be gracious to you, show you His favor, and give you His peace. Numbers 6:24-26.

The aunts' prayer over her the day she'd left The Haven made her wince. God's face hardly radiated with joy because of her now. Except maybe in embarrassment.

Victoria's hand slid to her stomach. Her fingertips probed, trying to feel some sensation that spoke of a baby nestled inside. She felt nothing physically. But deep in her heart, awe blossomed. That she was now responsible for another life brought tears to her eyes.

And yet—the aunts would want their young guests to be taught about God's love, to see it reflected in the staff. Victoria had messed up so badly; she felt unworthy of preaching to anyone. She'd face dismay and revulsion in people's—Ben's—eyes when they realized that she hadn't followed the Godly precepts she'd been raised on, hadn't walked her talk.

He'd be disgusted when he found out she wasn't the worthy daughter he thought.

Why did Ben's opinion matter so much?

"Good morning." Ben had been at The Haven for six days. He no longer doubted his theory that Victoria was pregnant.

Each morning, when he arrived in the kitchen, she was there, pasty-faced, desperately trying not to show her nausea, though she didn't race from the room as she had before. He knew why. He'd seen her outside, before the sun rose, and figured she was trying to get the worst of her morning sickness out of the way while she walked alone through the cold, snowy world. When she returned, she was always pale yet composed, munching on a stash of crackers she kept in a container on the counter. She acted as if she thought no one noticed.

But Ben noticed and he felt a strong sympathy for her. In fact, he couldn't stop thinking about Victoria and her baby, couldn't stop wondering how a strong woman like her had wound up pregnant and unmarried. This morning was no different. His heart raced at seeing her standing in front of the massive gas range, stirring scrambled eggs as if it was what the two of them always did on Sunday morning.

Dream on, Ben.

"Good morning. Church today," Tillie announced as she and Margaret came sailing into the kitchen.

"I think I might stay home today, Aunties." Victoria slid fluffy eggs onto a platter, set it in the middle of the big round table. She added buttered toast and a carafe of coffee.

"My dear, are you still unwell?" Though she ducked, Victoria couldn't avoid Margaret's palm on her forehead. "You don't feel warm."

"I'm fine. Just lethargic. I think I need to rest." Victoria set a glass of milk in front of Mikey, smiled and ruffled his hair.

"Perhaps you shouldn't have gone for such a long walk this morning then, dear." Tillie sat, placed her napkin in her lap and bowed her head. Silence fell as she said grace aloud. Then she looked directly at Victoria. "I'm sure you'll feel better once the service begins."

Ben smothered his smile when Victoria exhaled. Weak, timid old ladies? Hardly.

"You'll come along, too, Ben." Margaret nodded at his start of surprise. "You can sit in the front seat of the car. There's plenty of legroom."

Thus, when breakfast ended and the kitchen was restored to order, they all attended the local church. Inside the white-steepled structure, Ben silently commiserated with Victoria's reluctant presence, while obediently sitting where indicated, next to the ladies. Victoria was dispatched to escort Mikey to the children's service upstairs. When she didn't slide onto the pew next to him until the congregation was well into the first hymn, he knew she'd taken her time returning. She managed a smile when the pastor welcomed her back and nodded at those who turned to glance at her.

But Ben knew Victoria longed to be anywhere but here. In fact, during the minister's sermon on the love of God, he happened to glance at her down-bent head and saw her dab at her eyes several times, accompanied by a sniff.

Strong, capable Victoria was crying. Why did that make him feel so helpless? Why did he want to comfort her? She wasn't his responsibility and yet this plucky woman's distress tugged at his heartstrings. He intrinsically knew that she'd lost at love, that what she'd hoped for had not come to fruition and that, besides leaving her job, she'd left behind the guy who held her heart. The guy who was the father of her child. Yet, as far as Ben knew, she'd still told Tillie and Margaret nothing. Why?

As they rose to sing the closing hymn, Ben glanced at his hosts. Couldn't these usually astute ladies see that something was wrong? That the young woman they'd raised was desperately unhappy?

But as they chatted with friends in the foyer, on the ride home and all through lunch, Tillie and Margaret seemed oblivious to Victoria's distress. They giggled at Mikey's knock-knock jokes as if all was well.

When the two seniors finally left for an afternoon nap and Mikey was engaged in a Disney movie on television, Ben couldn't remain silent any longer.

"Why don't you tell your aunts you're pregnant, Victoria?" he asked baldly, hating the way she winced at the word.

"How do you know—it isn't—you don't understand." She shoved a handful of dark hair away from her face and picked at invisible threads on her jeans.

"What's to understand? You're going to have a baby." Ben shrugged. "You're not the first single woman to do that and you won't be the last. Life happens."

"Unmarried motherhood doesn't happen to girls Tillie and Margaret taught to revere God and keep His principles," she shot back, her voice shaky. "That's sin."

"I haven't been a Christian very long," Ben said, frowning at her. "But it seems to me that even David, a man after God's own heart, sinned. And God forgave him."

Her lack of response made him wonder if Victoria had even heard him. With her arms wrapped around her waist, she rocked slightly back and forth, her white face pinched with sadness and stained with tears. Beautiful but heartbreaking. And sort of remote.

"Victoria?" He touched her shoulder. "What about the baby's father?"

"He doesn't want me or the baby."

"Are you sure?" Ben found himself curious—too curious—about that answer.

"He doesn't want a child in his life. It would wreck his plan, weigh him down with responsibility for someone other than himself." She gave a tiny huff of laughter. "It took me five years and a ghastly mistake, but the one thing I finally realized about Derek is that he always ducks responsibility. He doesn't have the ability to see beyond his own needs."

Ben asked himself, *Am I ducking my responsibility to Mikey by asking for Tillie and Margaret's help to find the boy a new family? Am I doing it just to ease my own life?*

The answer required no thought. He was doing the only thing he could to ensure Mikey had a safe home with parents who could care for him. Ben had to believe that, in time, the couple would come to love Mikey as much as Neil and Alice had. As much as he did.

"I don't know what to do," Victoria whispered in a softly weeping voice Ben didn't think he was meant to hear.

Her sadness, grief, sorrow and worry touched his soul as little in recent years had.

"You're going to get on with your life," he told her firmly. "And I'm going to help you."

"Huh?" She stared at him as if he'd lost his mind. "How?"

"I have three months leave, Victoria. While Tillie and Margaret find Mikey a family, you and I are going to get the ball rolling on their plans for The Haven." He wondered where the idea had come from while mentally acknowledging that it was the least he could do to help the ladies who were helping him.

"But—but..." She gaped at him, unable to speak.

"You're a fixer, remember? You're smart, educated and you know how to get things done." Now he had a goal. He was good at goals, concrete plans that weren't like wildly swinging emotions. Ben felt more lighthearted than he had in eons. "You made a mistake, trusted a guy who wasn't worth it. But that's the past, Victoria. Now you're moving on."

"Meaning?" She frowned, dark head tilted to one side.

"Meaning you're going to be an awesome mom." He grinned. "But until then, you focus on making your aunts' project happen."

"I don't know." She didn't look convinced and she would have to be to fight through the obstacles that could stop her aunts' dream of a refuge for kids. "Maybe—"

"Listen, Victoria. Life gave you lemons. You met a jerk, got talked into something you shouldn't have and now you're home to regroup." Ben suddenly realized that he *wanted* to do this. With her. "Let us take your lemons and turn them into lemonade."

"Us?" Victoria stared at him, tears evaporating. A tiny smile flickered at the corner of her pretty mouth and spread across her entire face.

"Yes, you and me," he said firmly. She burst into laughter.

"You couldn't possibly know this, Ben, but lemonade is my absolute favorite drink." She held up her fist and when he stretched out his own, bumped her knuckles against his. "I think we're both nuts for even imagining their dream is possible, but—"

"We'll do it for the aunties," he said with a grin.

"And for me and you and Mikey." Victoria looked dazed.

"And for all the kids who'll come here to find a second chance," he reminded.

"Yes." She exhaled, pressed her shoulders back and nodded, as if to settle it in her mind. When she looked at him, he saw her chin lift in determination. "Thank you," she murmured.

Funny how that tiny smile she gave him took away the lingering pain in Ben's ribs and made his heart sing with anticipation.

He sure hoped he hadn't taken on too much with this offer to turn The Haven into the aunts' dream. But hadn't Tillie said that trusting God was an important step in becoming His child?

"I have no clue how this will work," he prayed later that evening. "What do I know about foster kids? But I can't do nothing. Victoria needs me. So I'm trusting You. Please help."

Ben stared out his window into the shadowy forest.

"Don't let me make another mistake," he added, suppressing the memory of another time when his attempt to help had ended in disaster.

Not again, Lord, his soul cried. *Never again.*

Chapter Four

Days later, Ben again found himself gazing at Victoria in admiration—until she caught him staring.

"Well?" she prodded, pushing back a hank of hair. "What do you think?"

"That you've accomplished a ton." He admired the way she'd smothered all her reservations about Tillie and Margaret's idea and simply got on with making their dream come true. "You're like a machine."

"Hardly." Victoria shrugged. "Once I, the aunts and their lawyers put the necessary insurance in place, it was a matter of proceeding to the next step." She stacked a sheaf of papers and slid them inside a folder on the massive oak desk. "That means drawing up an overall plan."

"Why don't I think you're totally convinced

this will work?" Ben muttered more to himself than her.

"Because I'm not." Her rose-toned lips pursed.

"And yet you'll go ahead with it anyway? Why?" But he knew. "Because you love them."

"Tillie and Margaret are my family. I'll do whatever they ask." Victoria arched her back in a stretch. "Which doesn't mean it'll be easy. We need all kinds of inspections and permits before we open, but none of that can happen until I can nail down what it is we want to do here. Right now, I'm stuck on activities we could offer." Her eyes fixed on him. "Any ideas?"

"It's a good thing I had to stay off my foot this week. Gave me plenty of time to think about that." Ben tugged a sheet of paper from his pocket, unfolded it and held it out. "Take a look. Some are only vague concepts so don't laugh."

"Why would I laugh? I'm relieved to hear any suggestions. Especially since my own seem so pathetic." Her gray eyes darkened with her frown. "It's weird but I remember very little about what my sisters and I *did* when we were kids here."

"Really?" Ben remembered way too much about his youth, mostly the constant feeling of drowning with fear that he'd mess up. And he had!

"What I do remember is how much fun we had, how we'd burst into laughter at the slightest provocation. Mostly I remember how happy we were." A nostalgic smile lifted Victoria's lips. After a moment, she shook off the past, scanned the paper he'd given her and blinked in surprise. "Snowshoeing, zip lining, ice fishing. These are great ideas."

"They're things I'd like to do if I lived here." Ben was flattered by her enthusiasm.

"Actually, offering activities like these should show anyone who questions us that The Haven has the ability to engage kids of all ages." She tapped her fingertip against her chin, scanning the list. "Most of these are probably novel to city kids. I think they'll dive right in. I just hope you'll still be around to lead them. I'm no wimp but I do not clean fish."

"As far as I know, Tillie and Margaret haven't had any offers yet so I guess we'll be here awhile, maybe even until my leave is over," Ben spoke softly, his gaze on Mikey who was busy with an antique train set Tillie had unearthed from the attic. "Fine by me. Whatever it takes to find the right family." He looked up to find a fierce frown marring Victoria's lovely face. "What?"

She swallowed hard then shook her head. Puzzled, he watched as she knelt beside Mikey and smoothed his hair before pressing a kiss against his forehead.

"You're such a cute little boy."

"I'm a *big* boy," he asserted, wrinkling his freckled nose.

Victoria agreed with a laugh, rubbed the heel of her hand against her eyelashes to dislodge the tears he'd glimpsed and then returned to her seat at the table. She waited until Mikey resumed train playing before speaking, her voice low, troubled.

"I know I've asked this before, Ben. But are you sure?"

"No. But it's the way it has to be, Victoria." He added, "Because I can't think of a better solution."

"Well, maybe we ought to start thinking in a different way." Victoria switched on the kettle before giving him an arch look. "From a more positive perspective."

"Huh?"

"You frequently say *can't*, Ben. *I can't do this. I can't do that.*" Her eyes sparkled. "Do you know the first verse my aunties taught me to memorize? 'I can do all things through Christ,'" she quoted.

"Tillie gave me that one to memorize, too," he admitted. "I guess I need to consider putting those words into action."

"Unca Ben?" Mikey stood in front of him, holding a book.

"What's up, Little Man?" Ben gathered his nephew on his knee and pressed a kiss against his head, loving the little-boy smell of him.

"This book is about Snow White," Mikey explained. He glanced at Victoria. "It's my favorite."

"I guessed that." She smiled and waited for him to continue.

"What's your question, kiddo?" Ben tickled him in the ribs until Mikey squealed with laughter. Boy, he would miss that sound.

"When Vic an' me go walkin' in the forest, c'n I see her?"

"Her, who?" Ben asked, absently noticing that his nephew needed new shoes.

"Snow White. She lives in the forest." Mikey slid off his knee and walked to Victoria. "With elves."

Ben smothered a laugh as Victoria said in her most serious voice, "You mean with the seven *dwarfs*?"

"Yeah. Them. So will I?" Mikey turned to look at him with utter trust in his eyes, just like Neil once had. That sent a shaft of pain straight to Ben's heart. He loved this kid so much. How could he just walk away from him?

"It's a fairy tale, honey," Ben heard Victoria explain. "That means it's just a story. It's not real. But we can pretend it is." She lifted him onto her lap and wrapped her arms around him, snuggling him close. "When I first moved here, I used to lie in the long, tall grass and pretend the animals from *The Jungle Book* were all around."

"Like lions and tigers?" Mikey's dark eyes stretched wide.

Victoria nuzzled Mikey's neck. "Exactly."

He giggled when Victoria mimed a roar then wiggled free and returned to his locomotive, happily chugging it over the metal rails.

"You're very good with him," Ben told her.

"I love kids. I never realized how much I've missed working with them." As if flustered by the admission, she began bustling around the kitchen as she made tea.

Ben sat, content to enjoy this side of the usually cool and collected Victoria. Somehow, watching her in such a domestic setting softened that air of determination she used like a shield. Here, now, she looked like someone's wife and a mother.

Where had that come from?

"Do Tillie and Margaret have candidates chosen as their first visitors to their 'retreat'?" Ben asked, trying to steer his thoughts away from Victoria Archer.

"I don't know." She turned from setting cereal treats on a plate to pin him with a mock-stern look. "I am not yet privy to the finer details. My job is to get things ready to go with flexibility for preteens." She set the plate on the table with a thud.

"Did your sister make these?" Ben asked after sampling one of the bars.

"I did. I told you. I am not inept when it comes to cooking." Her glare dared him to suggest otherwise.

"No, you're not. They're delicious." Ben quickly changed the subject. "Today you seem more, I don't know, up about the idea of turning The Haven into a retreat. How come?"

"At first it sounded ridiculous to me to even consider bringing kids way out here for some kind of mini-vacation," Victoria admitted. She set the steaming brown teapot on the table and added two cups. "But having seen the amount of prep work Tillie and Margaret have done and the number of official approvals they've already obtained, who am I to naysay it? Obviously a lot of people consider their idea plausible."

"And your—situation?" Having checked that Mikey's attention was still engaged with his train, Ben accepted his cup of tea before locking his gaze on her face, surprised by her softened expression. "Have you come to terms with that?"

"Didn't take much to adjust to my lifelong dream of motherhood." Victoria cradled her steaming cup, her glowing face making Ben envy her joy. Then she frowned. "It's just—I don't want to be an embarrassment to the aunts. I'm afraid they'll be disappointed in me."

"I doubt that could ever happen. They're so proud of you." He saw that didn't assuage her fears. "Victoria, I think I know how your aunts see God, but I'm curious about your view of Him."

"My *view*?" She sipped her tea, gray eyes narrowed as she searched the distance for an answer. "I guess I picture God as my Father. Maybe because I never had one. He gives advice through the Bible, guides me when I pray and listen to His voice. Like that." She shrugged, her expression sheepish. "I don't know if I can conceptualize God in appropriate words."

"A father figure is a pretty clear picture." Ben watched the fingers of one hand slip down and splay across her abdomen as she absently caressed it. She didn't realize what she was doing but the action made him wish he could help her shed the guilt and find some inner peace. Then maybe Victoria could enjoy her pregnancy as much as Alice had enjoyed hers. "Do you think God, your Father, would condemn you for a mistake? Are you waiting for Him to punish you?"

Her eyes widened before she slowly nodded.

"Why?"

"Because I deserve it." Her head dipped so her chin rested on her chest. "I broke His rules."

"You don't think the God of the universe, the Father who made you and understands everything about you, can forgive His own beloved daughter?" The pain that turned her gray eyes stormy reached out and squeezed his heart. "Or is it you who can't forgive yourself?"

"That's part of it," Victoria admitted, her voice whisper-soft.

"I'm still new at being a Christian, but one thing Tillie repeatedly reminded me of in her letters was that God forgives. If we ask."

From the way Victoria shifted in her chair, Ben guessed she needed time to think that through, so he crunched on another cereal bar and gazed out the big window at the impressive view of snow-capped mountains while she invited Mikey to enjoy a treat—which he did but immediately went back to his train.

"I'm blessed to have even a tiny part in the plans for this place," Ben murmured, hardly aware he'd voiced his thoughts until she gaped at him.

"You're a peacekeeper, Ben." Victoria's tone echoed her confused expression. "You've been part of lots of wonderful missions, protecting people all around the world."

"But this feels personal. Like I'm really involved and not just following orders. Which is kind of dumb because I'm not really involved at all, but—" He hesitated before admitting, "I wish I was. I wish I could be here to see the kids when they arrive and when they leave. See how

The Haven changes them. I'm a little envious that you'll get to witness that."

"Whoa! We haven't even got the program running yet," she cautioned with a laugh.

"You will," Ben assured her.

"You have that much confidence in us?"

He shook his head, his attention fixed on the way the sunbeam through the window enhanced Victoria's milky-pale skin and shiny dark hair. She was beautiful even when she frowned at him.

"You *don't* have confidence in us?" No mistaking that tart tone.

"I do have confidence in *you*," Ben clarified with a laugh. "But even more in God. With Him directing you, The Haven is going to be a smash hit." He chuckled at her dubious expression. "Anyway, you wouldn't accept anything else. Good enough isn't in your vocabulary, Victoria."

"That's true." She studied him for several moments before asking, "How can you know me so well when you've only been at The Haven for a week and I know so little about you?"

"Nothing to know. I'm boring." That intense stare of hers made Ben rise and top up their teacups, though he knew she wasn't going to let it go.

"Boring doesn't fit you at all, Blue Helmet." Victoria chuckled at his surprise. "You think I didn't know people nickname UN peacekeepers that because of their blue berets or helmets? I can read, Ben."

"Never doubted it for a moment." He finished his tea, oddly pleased that she'd bothered to learn about his work. "Just didn't think you were interested."

"I used to dream of visiting Africa as part of a missions group I sponsor. Sadly, I never managed to get there." Victoria made a face at her remaining tea, glanced at the coffeepot longingly, but finally gave a small shake of her head that he knew meant she wasn't ready to risk drinking it just yet. "Do you like being a peacekeeper, Ben?"

"Some days it's the best job in the world," he said quietly.

"And on the other days?"

"I'd like to scream with frustration." He smiled at her surprise. "Bambari in Central Africa was my last post. We were literally keeping the two sides apart, like a parent separating two squabbling children. The things people do to each other make me sick." He stopped, unwilling to immerse Victoria in the ugliness of hate.

"Yet you intend to go back to peacekeeping. Is that why you're anxious to see plans for The Haven succeed? Because it represents hope?" Victoria's astute comment made him realize she understood him better than she thought.

"Maybe. After everything that's happened—I

could use a little hope." Ben fell silent for a moment before shrugging off the grief to turn the focus back on her. "What's your next big hurdle?"

"Liability insurance, and then staffing. Which means firming up the activities we'll offer to start with." Victoria studied the notes in front of her a moment longer, then smacked them on the table. "I need to go for a walk. Wanna come along?"

"*Need to?* Because you've only been out walking twice already today." Ben swallowed his laughter as he put his mug in the dishwasher.

"Guilty." Victoria, face pink, turned away to hustle Mikey toward their coats. "I think best when I'm walking. Always have. Can you manage on your leg?"

"Sure." A week had made an amazing difference in his recovery, along with Victoria's insistence that he obey Chokecherry Hollow's doctor and not overdo things. Ben enjoyed her bossy overprotectiveness but relished the opportunity to test his ability to maneuver the uneven countryside. "I wish my rental car healed as easily as I do."

"Any word on that?" In her white parka, dark hair shining, Victoria looked like a snow princess, perfectly at home as they stepped into the winter wonderland outside. Mikey whooped with joy and raced ahead.

"The insurance company still has me on hold."

Ben grimaced. "They won't say when I can get the stuff I'd stored in the trunk, either."

"Stuff from Mikey's home?" When he nodded, she frowned. "I'd ask Jake to pick it up, but I'm not sure where the wrecker towed the car."

"Doesn't matter. They won't let me touch it until, in their language, a complete assessment has been done. All they say is wait, so I'll be dependent on you a while longer, I'm afraid." He hated feeling dependent. A new thought occurred. "Mikey and I must be in the way with all the changes you and your aunts are trying to make at The Haven. Jake should take us into Jasper to stay somewhere else."

Victoria burst into laughter, dark hair flying in the breeze. His stomach tightened at her attractiveness.

"Ben." She sounded as if she was remonstrating with a silly child. "This is high season in the Rockies. Ski time. Why waste your money?"

"But you're busy here. Maybe we could find a place in Chokecherry Hollow."

"A bed-and-breakfast? Why? Don't you feel welcome at The Haven?" she demanded, hands on hips.

"You and your aunts have been more than gracious. It's just—" Ben stopped, unable to say the rest, not when Victoria was staring at Mikey as if she wanted to scoop him into her arms and hold him like a mother bear protecting her cub. "I don't want to impose."

"You're not imposing. The aunts and I love having you and this guy." She bent down and hugged Mikey, who used her proximity to wash her face with a handful of snow. "You monkey!" Any other woman would have bawled the kid out but, as if it were hilarious to have a wet face in the cold, Victoria grinned and warned him, "When I catch you…"

Giggling, Mikey raced off, apparently unaware or uncaring that the dogs raced with him. Victoria paused and looked at Ben with the most beseeching gaze.

"I love that kid. Please don't take him away," she begged softly. "Not yet. Mikey's already lost so much. Let me spoil him, love him for a while longer."

"It will only make it harder for you both when he leaves," he warned. Wrong thing to say.

Victoria glared at him, lips pursed.

"So, it will be hard. Lots of things are hard. One thing I learned growing up with the aunts is that sometimes it's worth going through pain to experience life's best offerings." She got that dreamy look again, the one that told him she was thinking of her child so Ben said nothing to refute her comment.

"The aunts are meeting with a couple today," he murmured.

Victoria frowned. After a moment, she blinked, called out to Mikey and raced across the snowdrifts toward him.

Ben followed more slowly, mulling over her words, suddenly curious about the pain Victoria had suffered in the past and worried about what she would still face. Had she counted the cost of keeping her baby, the issues raising a child alone would bring?

But as he watched her and Mikey make snow angels, Ben knew it wouldn't matter. Victoria was the kind of woman who made up her mind to do something and then carried through. No matter what the cost to herself.

Which was just one of the many things he so admired about her.

As a friend, right?

Victoria couldn't tear her gaze away from the little boy studiously bent over the table. She smothered a smile as Mikey's chubby fingers contorted in a struggle to paste a lacy heart onto the poster paper they were turning into valentines.

"Tara, Thea and Enid are my Little Sisters in Edmonton. They are going to love these valentines, Mikey. Thank you for helping me."

"Welcome." He stopped for a moment and

lifted his head, dark eyes thoughtful. Clearly something was on his mind when he waited a long time before saying, "I maked Mommy special cards. I writed my name all by myself. Mommy liked that." He swallowed hard and bent his head. A single tear splashed onto his work. "No more cards," he whispered.

"Oh, yes, Mikey." Victoria rushed to correct him, desperate to help his little heart heal. "There will be lots of cards. We have to make a valentine for Uncle Ben, for sure, but not when he's around," she added in a whisper. She peeked over one shoulder, saw Ben standing in the doorway and pressed her finger against her lips in a shushing motion.

Mikey's dark eyes danced. He grinned as if she'd given him the best gift.

"What are you two whispering about?" Ben asked.

"It's a see-crud, Unca Ben. You can't hear."

Delighted to see the misery had vanished from Mikey's face, Victoria smiled at Ben as he poured a cup of coffee before sitting down beside her.

"How did the aunties' meeting go?" she asked.

"The couple is totally unsuitable." He complimented Mikey on his work then leaned back to drink his coffee.

"I'm sorry." Victoria felt compelled to say, but the truth was that she wasn't sorry. She was actually relieved that Ben struggled to find Mikey prospective parents, because some part of her kept hoping he'd realize he needed to parent his nephew himself.

"They'll find someone. They have to." The last was uttered almost desperately. He shook off his problems to ask, "Who are these for? Your sisters?"

"These are for my 'Little Sisters' in Edmonton." She glued as eagerly as Mikey.

"That must have been a huge time obligation, especially to young girls." Ben frowned at her. "You said you traveled a lot. How did you manage it?"

"You have to commit two to four hours per week, per girl," she agreed. "At first, it was a struggle. Three are actually true sisters, though they're in three different foster homes. The organization agreed that we could do things as a group so we got together at least once a week to have fun. But I also spent one-on-one time with each of them."

"Now you're here." Ben studied her, a frown wrinkling his tanned forehead. "How's that going to work?"

"I don't know. It's one of the things that makes staying at The Haven so difficult." *One* of the things. Her hand touched her stomach fleetingly.

"You still haven't told your aunts." It wasn't a

question. Ben wore a troubled look. "Victoria, you're not giving them a chance—"

"Don't," she begged quietly. When it seemed he'd argue she turned her attention to Mikey. "Very nice," she encouraged, hugging his tiny body close for a second before he wiggled away.

"C'n I ski?" he asked suddenly.

"Ski?" Victoria glanced at Ben, who looked as surprised as she was. "Why?"

"'Cause a boy in church tole me he skis with other kids an' he 'vited me." Mikey looked unsure for a moment, but then his chin thrust out. "Maybe he could be my friend?" he said wistfully.

"What a good idea. A smart boy like you can soon learn to ski." Belatedly Victoria looked to Ben for his approval and found him studying her with an intensity that made her uncomfortable. "Don't you think?"

"Uh, yeah. Skiing. Sure." Ben's gaze held hers for a second, slipped to her midriff then settled on Mikey. "We could do that, I guess."

Mikey jumped up and ran around the room cheering. Victoria stayed put, staring at her hands, unsettled by the expression she'd seen on Ben's face and her inner response to it.

He was a great guy. She liked him a lot. But

there could be nothing between them but friendship. She was going to be a mom.

Time was ticking. Soon Ben would leave.

Chapter Five

"Good, Mikey. You're doing great." Ben's breath caught in a rush of fondness as the boy grinned at him before resuming his concentration. If only…

For the third afternoon in a row, he and Victoria had taken Mikey to an area on The Haven's property with small undulating hills. Jake had groomed it so they could teach Ben's nephew the basics of negotiating on the ancient cross-country skis Tillie and Margaret had unearthed. Turned out, Mikey was a natural.

"Don't fall. Don't fall," Victoria said under her breath as she stood by Ben, watching Mikey maneuver the course they'd set.

"You've got it, son." Ben did a fist pump when Mikey reached the bottom of a little hill in the upright position. "Woohoo! Way to go."

"You called him son," Victoria murmured

pointedly. "You're very good with him." Why did she sound surprised?

"So are you." *Like a mother.* Ben shoved away the rush of appreciation. *Just friends, remember?* "Why wouldn't kids who visit The Haven enjoy this?" He loved the way her eyes lit up with anticipation. "Surely it wouldn't cost much to groom trails and I doubt there are any big insurance risks for cross-country skiing. You fall into soft snow."

"Plus, cross-country skiing is fairly low-cost and can be done almost anywhere. I also like that they'll learn a lifelong skill." Victoria's grin made her exhilaration obvious. A warm flush spread through Ben. He finally felt like he was contributing something to repay Tillie and Margaret's efforts to find Mikey new parents, and Victoria for the love she generously showered over the boy.

"I'll add skiing to the activity list." She smirked. "After I check with Jake. I'm not sure how he'll feel about having trail-grooming added to his list of duties. Not that he ever complains."

"Pretty sure Jake's one of the good guys." Ben glanced toward the small stone caretaker's cottage almost hidden in a grove of spruce trees. "What's his story, anyway?"

"I don't know." Victoria shrugged. "The aunties probably do but they've never shared. All I know is that Jake showed up at The Haven one day, sick and half-frozen. They took him in, helped him heal, offered him a job and he's been here ever since."

"A mystery man."

"He's very good to Tillie and Margaret and he always lets us girls know if there's an issue, though by the time we get here, he's usually taken care of what needs doing," she added with a smile. "The church family is very protective of them, too. You met Mrs. Marsh?"

"A very determined housekeeper. Refused to allow me to launder Mikey's and my clothes." Ben arched one eyebrow. "I think she believes I'll wreck the machines."

"She has her—"

"Standards," Ben finished with a chuckle. "So she's said. Repeatedly." He rolled his eyes at Victoria's amusement.

"Anyway, my aunts have many good friends nearby, but the reality is they're still alone in the boonies. For now." Victoria tossed him a frown. "Your talk with the aunts this time seemed to go long. Was there an issue?"

"The prospective parents they suggested interviewing aren't suitable. They already have their own family. Mikey would be competing. But I was actually detained by your Aunt Margaret and her computer." He didn't want to tattle but—

"Don't tell me she's downloading games again."

Exasperation colored Victoria's voice. "She always insists a new game is going to be better than the fifty she already has."

"Don't worry." Ben waved to Mikey who was skiing down an incline toward them and apparently loving it, if the grin on his face was any indication. "I sorted it out for her," he said.

"How?" Victoria frowned.

"Mostly I cleaned up the drives but it's still not very fast. Patience isn't your Aunt Margaret's strong suit, is it?" When Victoria snorted with laughter, he nodded. "That's why I suggested she buy a new computer, one that will run her games at the proper speeds."

"You didn't?" For the first time since she'd met him, Victoria ignored Mikey, who now skied toward them. Instead she glared at Ben. "Do you have any idea what you've done, Major?"

"No," Ben admitted, now completely confused and wishing he hadn't interfered. "What?"

"Thanks to you, Margaret is now going to want me to take her to Edmonton to shop for a new computer. The process will take days because she'll have to research each one to ensure she's getting the best deal." She closed her eyes and sighed. "Aunt Maggie researches everything. In that regard, she is very patient."

"But—"

"Tillie will want to come along. Quilt fabric is her weakness," she explained, her voice tight.

"But—" Ben bit his lip when she again interrupted.

"I'm supposed to get The Haven ready for this onslaught of kids. I don't have time to waste shopping in the city." Victoria shook her head. "I wish you'd talked to me before you suggested Aunt Maggie shop for a new computer, Ben."

"I didn't suggest she do that," he said loudly then felt a wash of shame as Mikey's eyes stretched in surprise. "No shopping trip is necessary. She picked one out online. It's already ordered," he added quietly.

"No shopping trip?" Victoria blinked. "Really?"

"Really. I set up a spreadsheet to compare different models. She studied it and chose one. We've also packed up a lot of the, er, junk that won't work with her new computer. We're going to take it to the seniors' center in town to see if they can use it." Ben gulped when Victoria threw her arms around him and hugged him as if he'd saved her life. He'd never particularly liked invasion of his personal space, but he liked her hug. "Don't thank me yet," he warned.

She stepped back, face wary. "Why?"

"Her new computer comes with a gift certificate for seven games." He waited, but Victoria only laughed.

"Good."

"That's it?" He couldn't believe it. "After reaming me out—"

"Sorry. I should be thanking you." Victoria's eyes sparkled, giving life to her pale face. After a moment, she asked in a troubled tone, "How do you feel about meeting new parents for Mikey? Are you hesitant? And what about when you have to explain it to him?"

"I'll make him understand," Ben assured her. *Somehow.* "I think your aunt feels her old board games might make her seem out of step with the younger generation."

He worried she wouldn't take the bait and change of subject when she gazed at him with that probing stare that made him nervous. Then she shrugged.

"I will gladly light the match to burn those old board games in a campfire, just to be rid of them." Victoria's eyes narrowed. "How do you come to know so much about computers, Major?"

"Daddy said Unca Ben's a 'puter genie," Mikey chirped.

"Genius," Ben corrected. "And I'm not."

"Daddy said." Mikey was firm. "Hey, c'n I ski over there?"

"You can go as far as that old burnt-out jack

pine tree, then turn around and come right back. Okay?" When the boy hurried away, Victoria turned back to Ben. "A computer genius, huh? And you let us think you're an ordinary peacekeeper," she chided.

"I am. Computers are just a hobby. Actually, computer *games* are my hobby. I make them up," he confessed.

"Really?" Victoria looked at him differently, but he couldn't tell if it was with admiration or because she thought he was some sort of tech geek. "Do tell, Ben."

"Not much to tell. There's a lot of downtime with peacekeeping, so I spend it playing with computers." Ben didn't want to reveal too much about his solitary life, though he could see questions building in Victoria's expressive eyes.

"How'd you get started?" she wanted to know.

"When they get off duty, most of the guys like to let off steam, relax by partying. I'm not much into that," he admitted and wondered if she found him boring. "I shared quarters with a guy, Brian, who spent a lot of time on his computer. Long story short—he got me started."

"That was nice. Do you still keep in touch?"

"Brian was killed on a mission." Ben didn't want to remember how he'd lost the best friend he'd ever had. Computers were much easier than emotions and relationships. "Turns out, I have more of an affinity with computers than I do with people."

"I don't believe that," she said firmly. "You're great with Mikey and the aunts."

"Thanks," Ben said, struggling not to feel too pleased by her compliment. "Anyway, Brian's the one who started me thinking about my future, about when I leave the military."

"Oh?" Victoria studied his face as if the answer lay there.

"Someday, I hope to open a little store to help people with their computer issues, kind of like I helped Margaret." Ben shrugged. "So far it's just a dream, but I'm socking away every spare dime in hopes of one day making it come true."

"I think it's a great idea." She waved at Mikey, who'd reached the designated tree, then turned her pensive gaze back on him. "No reason why you couldn't start your business now, is there, Ben? Then you could stay in Canada and raise Mikey."

As if he hadn't thought of that. And rejected it.

"You can't?" Victoria's frown demanded an explanation.

"I don't have enough saved to withstand the first few years of building a business. That's something a lot of start-up small businesses don't plan for—the first few lean years of getting established are risky. I need to have lots of reserves and I don't. Yet."

"Hmm." She studied him for a moment in that way he recognized as an internal debate on whether or not to speak her mind.

"Say it," Ben said, heart sinking. He just knew she was going to bug him again about keeping Mikey, and he was already having second and third thoughts about his plan to find the boy a good home. Yet inside his deepest heart, he knew he couldn't be Mikey's dad. It wasn't just the lack of money—it was the lack in him.

"The aunts would have my head for asking such an indelicate question, but—" Victoria paused then blurted, "Did Mikey's parents have insurance?"

"Yes. A little. But that's for his future. College, to buy a home, whatever he wants." He had to squelch the speculation he saw rising in her eyes. "I'm not touching it."

"Not even to keep Mikey with you?" she asked softly.

"No." Ben shook his head. "Anyway, I don't believe having me as a parent is his best option."

"He loves you, Ben."

"I know that. And I love him." He wanted to change the subject so Victoria wouldn't see how desperately he wished he could be the kind of parent Mikey needed.

"You're all he has now." Her whispered comment struck straight at Ben's heart, but he shoved away the pain with grim determination.

"I know. Poor kid. That's exactly why I need to find him a better option," he said. "Nobody should be stuck with me as their parent. I learned that long ago." Turning away, he beckoned to Mikey. When the boy skied up to them, he asked, "Are you cold?"

"Nope."

"Then let's go for a walk. I want to test out my ankle." A sense of loss almost overwhelmed Ben as Mikey quickly agreed. While he freed the boy of his skis, he wondered how many more chances he'd have to spend with his nephew before relinquishing his care to someone else. "Aren't you coming with us?" he asked when Victoria hoisted the skis to one shoulder and turned toward the house.

"No. I'll take these back to The Haven and make us some cocoa. You guys go ahead."

As Ben watched her walk away, he was aware of a growing distance between them. Had he disappointed her? Victoria's opinion had come to mean a lot in the short time he'd known her. He wanted to see approval on her lovely face—approval for him. He wanted that very badly.

But not enough to risk Mikey's future.

Maybe if she knew what…no. That memory was too ugly to share with anyone.

What was with Ben, anyway?

Victoria plodded through the snow toward The Haven, struggling to accept his refusal to stay and raise Mikey.

"Can't You do something?" she prayed aloud. "It isn't right that Mikey will be raised by someone else when he and Ben love each other so much."

But as usual, it seemed her prayers hit an impenetrable ceiling. She had a hunch there was something else going on with Ben, something more than his feelings of inadequacy to the task of fatherhood. Something that added to the burden he carried about his brother. But what?

Frustrated, Victoria stored Mikey's skis in the garage and went inside. Tillie and Margaret sat at the big kitchen table, snuggling steaming mugs.

"How did the skis work?" Margaret asked as she poured Victoria a cup of cocoa.

"Great. I don't know how Jake got such a great trail made." She shed her outdoor gear, accepted the cup and sat down, too.

"Ben helped him create some sort of gizmo he attaches to the snowmobile. It's quite ingenious," Margaret mused.

"Are you all right, dear?" Tillie asked. "You looked troubled when you came in."

Victoria decided to probe. Her aunts had a gift for learning what was in the hearts of the service men and women to whom they wrote.

"Ben loves Mikey. I can't figure out why he feels compelled to find him another family. Why doesn't he want to raise Mikey himself?"

"Why don't you ask him?" Tillie said, but she didn't look at Victoria.

"I did. All he says is that he won't make a good father because he failed his brother." The aunts' placid faces gave nothing away, so she pressed on. "But his brother straightened up, built a life for himself. He got past his mistakes. So why can't Ben now be the father his nephew needs?"

"We can't answer that, dear." Tillie rose and placed her cup in the dishwasher. When she turned to face Victoria, tears glittered on her eyelashes. "You have to ask Ben."

"Oh," she whispered, heart pinching at her aunt's tender heart.

"Get him to talk about his work overseas," Margaret suggested. She rose, wrapped her arm around her sister's waist and together they walked from the room. "Let's work on a crossword, sister. That always helps soothe the heart."

"Why overseas?" Victoria frowned at the dogs curled up on the floor on top of a heat register. "I thought Ben said he couldn't parent Mikey because of his brother."

She was so lost in her questions about handsome Ben that she was startled when the back door opened and Ben and Mikey burst inside.

"I saw a deer, Vic! It was he-uge." Mikey almost tore off his snowsuit in his excitement. "I gotta tell Miss Tillie and Miss Margaret. Where are they?"

"In the study, I think." Victoria smiled as he raced from the room. "He's a bit excited."

"You think?" Ben hung up the clothing, removed his boots and then padded to the table. A shake of the carafe made him smile. "Just what I need." He poured a mug of cocoa and sat down across from her. "You looked pensive when we came in. Anything wrong?"

Victoria was about to deny it when she had second thoughts. She could at least ask Ben about his work.

"I was just thinking. You said you were posted in Africa?" She watched him nod as her brain chose and discarded words to ask what she desperately wanted to know. "Can you tell me about it?"

"Why?" He frowned, blue eyes turning navy.

"So I'll know something about what you do." She ducked her head, pretending to study the contents of her almost-empty mug. "You stand guard, is that it?"

"Among other things." Did he relax just a little? "It's not glamorous or exciting, Victoria. It's day after day of trying to keep the peace."

"But what's it like?" she pressed, realizing she really did want to know. "Are there families living there? Are there kids?"

Ben winced. "Both," he muttered.

"It's always the most helpless that suffer in war, isn't it?" she said. "Talk to me, Ben."

"Bambari is a town in the Central African Republic. The United Nations Peacekeeping force is tasked with the protection of civilians and also supports the transition process to new government, facilitates humanitarian assistance, promotes and protects human rights, disarmament, reintegration and repatriation processes." He stopped, looked at her and then gulped. "Sorry. That's the official line we're told to give."

"Sounded like it." Something told Victoria to keep him talking. "Is it very hot most of the time?"

"It's warm, but mostly it's muggy and frequently cloudy. December and January are the most comfortable." Was Ben becoming less tense?

"The official language is French, right?" At his nod she asked, "So you're bilingual?"

"I'm fully fluent in French and English, but I can get by in several languages. Turns out I have a facility for them," he said in a self-deprecating tone. What a lot she didn't know about this intriguing man.

"What do you like best about Bambari?" Victoria held her breath, hoping he wouldn't shut down as shadows crossed his face.

"The people. Their smiles. The kids—" He stopped, clamped his lips together.

"Aunt Tillie and Aunt Margaret had a soft spot for the kids they ministered to in Africa, too. Watch out if anyone hurt one of them. My aunties are tigers for kids."

"I know." Something was wrong. Victoria could tell from the muscle flickering in Ben's rock-hard jaw.

"What did I say?" She reached out and covered his fisted hand with her fingers. "What's wrong, Ben?" He didn't respond, so she let go, cleared her throat and said, "You know my secret. Can't you confide in me?"

He lifted his head and stared at her for a very long time. Victoria had almost given up hope, when he finally spoke.

"His name was Issa." Ben's face was inscrutable. "I think he was about six years old."

She said nothing, held her breath and prayed he'd continue.

"We were on patrol when I spotted him under an acacia tree." Ben's mouth tightened. "He was dying of starvation."

Victoria drew in her breath, aghast at the thought.

"I carried him to the hospital." For a moment, a spark lit Ben's blue eyes. "They kept him for several months, and he began to thrive."

"That's great." But Victoria knew there was more.

"He was such a sweet kid. I was concerned about finding his family so I visited him as often as I could. When I learned his family had all been killed in the civil war, I started to bring him things—a little toy to amuse him, a shirt to replace his ruined one, whatever he needed. The day Issa finally spoke to me was a big deal. We became real pals."

Ben cleared his throat and blinked several times. He seemed riveted by something outside the window but she knew it was a facade, a space of time to find the control he seldom lost.

"Tell me what happened, Ben," she begged when it seemed he'd never speak again.

"There were so many kids to treat. When Issa was deemed healthy enough, they sent him about seventy miles away to a camp for displaced persons, to make room for other sick children." His voice choked up. He paused before continuing. "I did all I could but Issa was taken away. The only thing I had time to do was slip him a few francs."

"But Issa was fed at the camp, right? Taken care of?" Victoria didn't like Ben's sideways glance.

"You'd think so." He simply stared at her.

"Something bad happened." Her throat tightened. "Tell me."

"I tried hard to keep track of Issa, to make sure he was being cared for." Ben pushed away his mug. "He knew how to read a little so I wrote to him. I never heard back. I wasn't allowed to visit the camp, either. All I could do was pray for him."

"Oh, Ben." Victoria's heart ached for the situation he'd been in and for the child she knew he'd loved.

"One day, Issa appeared at our base. He'd walked for days to see me. He was so thin and bedraggled, but he was so proud. He had a gift for me." A heartbreaking smile filled with sadness flickered across his lips. "He could barely stand up on his thin little legs, but he'd brought *me* something." Ben's voice cracked. He took a minute to recover before continuing. "I insisted he eat something before I opened it. I was on my way back to him with food when an explosive device went off. Issa was killed."

"Oh, no." She covered her mouth with her

hand, aghast and only too aware of Ben's pain. "I'm so sorry."

"Me, too." He knotted his fingers together as he spoke, his voice harsh. "An investigation determined someone had hidden a bomb in the basket Issa made for me. It's my fault Issa died."

"No, Ben. You weren't to blame—"

"There was a rebel faction in the camp. I'm sure Issa told them about my letters, probably read my promise that someday I'd come for him. They don't like outsiders, especially outsiders who talk about taking away their kids." Ben's face was haggard. "Someone in that camp befriended him, taught him to make reed baskets, encouraged him to sneak out of the camp and find me, to give me a gift as a thank-you. They wanted to kill me."

She couldn't say a word, couldn't stop him. She didn't want to. Ben needed to get it said, but his next words stunned her.

"Instead Issa paid with his life. They used a little boy to inflict pain. It's my fault he died. I wasn't a newbie. I knew there were bad people who'd use anyone—even a little boy." She shook her head vehemently but he ignored her. "They were my letters, Victoria. If I hadn't written to Issa, he might still be alive."

"But—why?" she asked, unable to understand. "Why do such a thing?"

"Hate doesn't need a reason," he rasped. "You learn pretty early when you're in the military that hate-mongers try to ease their own pain by causing others to suffer. But that doesn't excuse me."

"Ben." Victoria rubbed a hand over her eyes.

"I'm responsible. Do you understand now why I can't take a chance with Mikey? Some father I'd make," he scoffed. "I've already wrecked too many lives. I can't mess up any more. All my *help* ever does is wreck people's lives. I won't do that to Mikey."

"But your brother broke free of his past," she protested.

"Did he?" Ben made a face. "Neil had flashbacks, Victoria. Horrible nightmares, long after the drugs were gone from his system. The doctors said he might always have them. If only I'd done better, been more careful, maybe I could have—"

"Stop it, Ben." It was so hard to chastise him, especially after what he'd just told her. But Victoria wasn't going to let this wonderful man drown in *if onlys*. "Do you know Aunt Margaret's life verse? 'God works all things together for good for His children.' We can't always know why. That's where trust comes in."

"Trust and not repeating your mistakes." Ben rose slowly, studied her for a moment. Then he said in the gentlest voice, "I wish I could raise Mikey, Victoria. He's a great kid, and I love him a lot. But that's exactly why I don't believe I'm the right person to oversee his future. Everyone I love ends up dead. I won't risk that with Mikey. I have to get out of his way, let someone who knows what he's doing be his parent."

Then he walked out of the kitchen, a lone, solitary figure who'd just broken her heart with the saddest story she'd ever heard.

"Ben's Your child," she whispered. "He can't go on carrying this load of guilt. Please show me how to help him."

Chapter Six

"I'm sorry, ladies, but this couple just isn't suitable for Mikey."

"But they're educated, settled—" Tillie lifted her hands palm upward in frustration.

"I know, but I can't get past their list of rules. Sorry." Ben needed escape, so he thanked them and left to coax Victoria outside to visit the spot he and Mikey had found, a spot he knew would be perfect for a zip line.

"Jake told me there's a small meadow under the snow down there. No treetops to snag potential zip liners. No jagged rocks to catch on their clothes." He studied her face. Was she less pale this morning? "Also, if zip-lining in the winter, the kids could even drop off into the snow if it was deep enough."

"Maybe let's *not* suggest that, okay?" She rolled her eyes. "But the site's perfect." The white cloud of her breath mixed with his. "What was the couple you interviewed today on Skype like?"

"Unsuitable." A little off balance by the question, Ben decided to tell the truth. "They aren't the kind of parents I want for Mikey."

"Because?"

"They've already made a list of rules for him to adhere to, with punishments. And they don't like to travel." Ben figured he probably sounded ridiculous but there were certain things he wouldn't bend on.

"Travel?" Victoria perched on a boulder and stared at him.

"Silly, right? But I want Mikey to take trips with his family, to see God's creation, broaden his appreciation for life." It sounded silly when he said it out loud.

"Ben," she began hesitantly. "Aunt Maggie is worried they won't be able to find exactly what you want. She thinks you're hoping for a couple who are identical to Mikey's parents. Are you?"

There was one sure thing about Victoria. She was blunt. Ben liked that about her. You knew exactly where you stood with Victoria. She didn't pretend.

"Maybe not *exactly*," he said with a frown.

"Well, they're not giving up. They're still searching and asking God to lead them to the right person for Mikey." Victoria heaved a snowball at him that he just managed to duck.

"Hey!"

"Just testing the consistency of the snow," she said with a chuckle and jumped to her feet. "It's perfect for making a snow fort."

"You must be feeling better." Ben glanced around. "A fort here?"

"Right here," she confirmed. "I need to work up an appetite for dinner. Tillie's making her special barley soup in the slow cooker and Aunt Maggie is making fresh rolls. They're both fabulous cooks."

"How are *you* doing, Victoria?" he asked. "Really, I mean?"

He couldn't help but note the unconscious flutter of her hand across her midsection.

"You mean with their plans for The Haven?" Victoria avoided his eyes and began energetically piling snow to form walls. "Things are coming together. If we intend to make Canada Day their grand opening, we'll need to start advertising for staff. On a frosty day like today, July First seems a long way off, but it will be here before you know it."

"How many staff do you think?" Ben followed her lead and packed snow.

Her phone interrupted a litany of logistics.

"Didn't think I'd get coverage up here. Excuse

me." She frowned at the caller ID. "It's my Little Sister. Hi, Tara. What's up?"

By the way her brow furrowed, Ben knew this call was serious so he eavesdropped without compunction.

"Honey, Thea wouldn't run away to come here. Anyway, I doubt she even knows where The Haven is. Have you spoken to your foster worker?"

Ben's stomach took a nosedive at the words and his concern grew when Victoria hung up from that call and immediately dialed someone she called Enid, apparently Tara and Thea's sister. He admired the way she sought to ease the girl's fears when it was clear to him that her own were mushrooming.

"It will be okay, honey," Victoria soothed, though something told Ben she wasn't sure it would be. He figured that was because Victoria knew there were too many things a rebellious almost-teen could get into. "I promise I'll watch out for Thea. You and Tara keep praying, okay? God will work this out."

When she finally hung up, Victoria bowed her head, obviously sending her own plea for God's protection of the missing girl.

"What?" Ben asked when she lifted her head.

"Thea, one of my Little Sisters, is being bullied at school. Apparently she was humiliated today and ran away. Her sisters believe she's on her way here." She interpreted the look on his face and nodded. "The authorities have been alerted."

"So, we'll watch for her to show up," Ben soothed.

"If only I'd been in Edmonton. It would be so much easier for Thea to find me there."

"Who was it who recently scolded me about *if onlys*?" he reminded.

"Me," she agreed absently, shook out her mitts and pulled them back on. "Let's go back to The Haven and drive down the road, just in case Thea's on the way." She climbed onto the snowmobile.

"Good idea," Ben agreed.

"Your leg—"

"Is fine after all the mollycoddling I've received."

"Not from me." Victoria frowned at him. "I don't even know what that means."

"To mollycoddle, as in to pamper, coddle, spoil," Ben clarified as he climbed on behind her.

Victoria might not admit to mollycoddling him but she drove like a turtle over rocky bumps and hillocks until they reached the main road. He scanned the road with her but the winter sun was hidden behind a cloud and with light snow now falling, it was difficult to see any distance.

"I can search the road if you're tired," he offered when they stopped at a high spot.

"That's nice of you, Ben, but I have to do this. I feel responsible," she admitted.

"How can you be responsible?" He dismounted, found a little higher elevation and surveyed the area. Nothing.

"Because I'm here when I should be where they can reach me if they need to." He could almost see the guilt settling on her shoulders. "Tomorrow, I'll contact the organization and ask them to find someone else to be their Big Sister."

"You actually think this Thea will try to come here?" Ben frowned at Victoria's nod. "But The Haven is a long way from Edmonton."

"Thea is just stubborn enough to try it." Victoria bit her bottom lip. "She's also very angry at me."

"Why?"

"Thea sees my not being there for her and her sisters as a kind of betrayal. I promised I'd be there when they needed me, and I'm not. But—" She heaved a sigh.

"But you have to be here for your aunts now," he finished. "She won't understand?"

"Maybe." Victoria didn't sound convinced. "Thea's had a lot of disappointment in her life. She doesn't trust easily."

"But she trusted you." When she nodded, Ben said, "So where's *your* trust, Victoria?"

She frowned, twisted to stare at him. "What do you mean?"

"You told the girl who phoned to trust God." A faint smile tilted his mouth. "Practice what you preach, Big Sister."

She caught her breath at his impudence then released it in a burst of laughter.

"You don't mince words, do you? But you're right." Victoria stood beside him, peering through the lowering gloom. He figured she was afraid they'd find Thea trudging toward them, but more afraid they wouldn't.

Ben wanted to go back. He was cold and his leg hurt, but more importantly, he didn't like the defeat he could see in her eyes. "She's not on this road, Victoria."

"No, she isn't." Without argument, she turned the snowmobile around and drove them back toward The Haven. Once there, she climbed off and stumbled. He saw a tear dangling on the end of her lashes.

"You have a very big heart, Victoria."

"Anyone would be concerned about a missing girl," she mumbled in a half sob before stumbling again.

"Not everyone would go looking for her." He slid his hand over hers and squeezed. "You're going to be great with kids who come to The Haven. And you'll make a wonderful mother."

"I hope so," she whispered.

"But you're going to have to make a break with the past," Ben added gently.

"I did that when I left Edmonton," she shot back. She frowned when he shook his head. "What do you mean?"

"Victoria," he chided gently. "These three sisters you befriended clearly need constant contact and you're no longer in a position to give it. You're way out here instead of in the city where they can run to you."

"I know," she agreed, hating the thought of failing these girls she loved. "I said I'd call but I won't just cut them off."

"If you don't, how are they going to accept someone else, another Big Sister?" he asked quietly. Then, "Is that why you're keeping your apartment?"

Victoria blinked in surprise, glad he was still holding her hand as she slipped on an icy patch. "How—"

"I didn't mean to eavesdrop this morning. I was getting a cup of coffee and didn't realize you were in the next room." His solemn gaze studied her. "You didn't give your landlord notice, just told him you'd be away. Is that because you intend to go back to the city, because you believe you might have a chance with the baby's father? Are you hoping—"

"No."

Why was he so relieved that she didn't even consider it?

"Derek was a mistake and that's over. It's just—moving feels overwhelming right now. I'm so tired. I can't face packing up all my stuff," Victoria sighed, apparently accepting reality. "But you're right. I do need to make the trip and tie up my loose ends. Soon."

"I could help, if you want. As a small repayment for all you've done for us." He smiled at her dubious glance.

"Really?" She looked hopeful, as if she wanted his help. "You have no idea what a pack rat I am."

"Doesn't matter." He tried to hide his painful memories. "Recently I've gained some packing experience with Neil and Alice's stuff." He shook off the introspection. "Just let me know when."

"Thank you, Ben," she said with feeling.

"Sure."

Too aware of Victoria's small hand folded in his, Ben released it. Immediately a sense of loss engulfed him. The mountain darkness seemed to descend like a shroud, blocking out everything but the welcoming lights of The Haven. It was as if he, too, was lost, searching for a place to belong. A home. With Victoria striding ahead, it felt he'd suddenly lost a sweet and lovely connection, a tender sharing he'd seldom found before.

Ben figured he'd better forget that because he wasn't staying. He couldn't. His purpose in coming here was to figure out the future for his nephew. Despite continued misgivings, Ben still couldn't see an alternative. He wasn't a father. He made the wrong decisions too often to take on raising an innocent child. He loved Mikey. He wanted the best for him. That meant finding someone who knew what a child needed. Someone like Victoria with her tender heart and giving spirit. She had a mother's heart. She'd know how to raise Mikey.

If only he could be around to watch it.

"Get your head on straight, soldier," he muttered to his reflection in his bedroom mirror. "Victoria's amazing, but she's already got her hands full. She can't take on your problems, too."

But as he answered Tillie's call to come for supper, Ben couldn't help noticing how Mikey responded to Victoria's loving touch, how her face softened when she gazed at his nephew. He also couldn't help his accelerated heart rate when her gray eyes found his and a sweet smile curved her lips.

She can only ever be a friend, his brain chided.

Funny but Victoria already seemed like a lot more than just a friend.

* * *

Two days later, Victoria entered the workshop and saw Ben and Jake intensely focused on something Ben was holding.

"So, what do you think?" Ben said to Jake, apparently unaware that she'd entered the building.

"That's a fine piece of work." Jake slid one fingertip across the smooth surface before standing back to admire it. "You have a natural aptitude for woodworking."

"I haven't done it since high school, but it felt good to make something out of those scraps you gave me." Ben studied the wood remnants. "I think your suggestion for making a cover is doable before Valentine's Day."

A cover for what? Victoria wondered.

"Valentine's? That's soon."

"I know. It's a gift for Victoria," Ben said in a voice she had to strain to hear. "To say thank you from Mikey and me for all she's done."

"Ah." Jake nodded.

Victoria's heart thumped. How could she announce herself now? She'd spoil a surprise Ben had worked so hard on. She stayed where she was and waited for the right moment to slip out.

"Thank you for your help, too, Jake."

"Any time. The tools are ancient, but they're top notch and still work fine." Jake surveyed the room. "The place has most everything a guy needs to create."

"Have you used it often?" Ben asked.

"I wish. There's always another job to be done around here. Keeps me pretty busy." Jake turned away to continue sharpening a hoe. "Margaret wants a larger garden come spring so I'll need this ready."

"Do you think their idea of a foster retreat will work?" Ben asked.

Victoria leaned in to hear the response.

"The ladies will put everything they have into trying. As will their girls." Jake sounded happy.

"Girls? But only Victoria's here," Ben protested.

"For now." Jake returned to his work. "The others will be back."

"How do you know?" Ben asked.

"Tillie and Margaret were missionaries for a long time. They got in the habit of thinking about others. They raised their foster daughters the same way."

"I'm not sure what you mean."

"You know Adele's a chef?" Jake waited for Ben's nod. "On her day off, she cooks at a food kitchen to feed the homeless. Olivia isn't military but she works for them. *By the book* is her middle name. She's always in control, except in the hospital ward in Ottawa, when she holds drug babies who are going through withdrawal." He frowned at Ben. "Don't spread that around. I only found out by accident."

"Right." Ben paused. "Victoria's part of the Big Sister program."

"Anything to do with kids, that's Victoria." Jake returned to work.

Victoria blushed, knowing it was true.

"There's a fourth sister, isn't there?" Ben asked.

"Gemma. She's a tour guide to exotic places." Jake paused, stared into the distance. "When she's not traveling, tour companies pay her to speak about their tours. She donates that speaking fee to Habitat For Humanity. She likes nothing better than hands-on helping."

Victoria thought there was something about Jake's words that seemed private, as if they'd been pulled from him.

"Why would Gemma come back here?" Ben wondered aloud.

"Don't know yet. But she will." Jake turned away.

Guilt suffused Victoria over eavesdropping. She slammed the door then stomped her feet.

"Hello? Anyone here?"

"Over here," Ben called. "Talking about you." He laughed at her arched eyebrow. "Jake was just saying you and your foster sisters are all givers, like your aunts."

"They are. That's why their idea for The Haven will succeed," Jake murmured. "Also because it's a good idea."

"I dropped Mikey off at his new friend, Garnet's, house." Victoria noticed the gift Ben and Jake had been talking about had disappeared. "The aunts have gone to a ninetieth birthday party. They'll pick up Mikey on the way home."

"This afternoon's gonna be quiet without everyone around. I don't like that. I think too much." Jake's voice held a dark, haunted quality. "Guess I'll go chop some firewood."

"Let me know if I can help," Ben said. "I'd rather work than sit around any day."

"Appreciate that," Jake said and grinned at Victoria. "I have a hunch that's why this one's stopped by. Heard she intends to throw a thank-you dinner for all the volunteers who helped us out with the cabins. We must have had over forty Chokecherry Hollow folks show up to help. Big dinner. See you." He left.

Over forty people? Victoria hadn't realized there'd be so many when the aunts suggested a party.

"Not that I doubt you can do it," Ben said as they trudged through the snow back to the main house. "You have an overdose of gritty determination. But how do you go about feeding that many people?"

"Lots and lots of help." Victoria grimaced at her squealing phone. Then she smiled. "It's Adele. Hey, Sis. Next Thursday?" She shrugged out of her coat, smiling her thanks at him before checking the pile of papers stacked on the table. "Next Thursday works. Over forty, Jake thinks. Nobody cooks like you, Adele. If you're sure you can—really?"

She couldn't help grinning like a kid as her sister laid out her plans. Catching Ben's scrutiny, she winked at him, elated that she wouldn't have to manage on her own. "Ben will help me with all that. If you can manage the menu, I'll be thrilled. Just let me know what you need. Thank you, Sis."

Victoria sobered at Adele's questions about the missing Thea, the knot in her stomach twisting tighter.

"Nobody's seen her. She hasn't shown up here, and I'm getting really worried. Where could she be? Yeah, I'll keep praying." Judging by Ben's face, when she completed her phone call, he'd drifted off into some world far away from The Haven. "Hey." Victoria nudged his shoulder. "Are you okay?"

"Yes." But he looked sad. "I was listening to you and thinking that's what I miss most about losing Neil and Alice. There's nobody to share with anymore, even if we did mostly communicate through email and texts." He shrugged. "About this party. Ever heard of overdoing?"

"Yes, but I'll be fine. And you can always share family with me." She blushed under his intense regard before bending her head and shuffling papers. "Anyway, I really want to do this for the aunts. Everyone's been so kind and helpful to them."

"It's also the perfect opportunity to announce The Haven's newest venture to the community. So tell me what I can help with."

Overly aware of the big, smiling soldier seated across from her, Victoria outlined Adele's dinner plan.

"Wow! That's no half-baked, spur-of-the-moment meal," he said. "Sorry. What I should say is I admire how considerate you're being, showing appreciation to people who are important to Tillie and Margaret. I like how you tackle everything with a give-it-my-best attitude, even if it means going above and beyond. I'll gladly help."

Victoria blushed even darker at this praise, glad that Ben was too busy making a list of details to notice her burning cheeks. They were discussing the buffet when someone knocked on the back door.

Hope simmered as Victoria jumped to her feet and raced to throw open the big oak door, Ben hot on her heels. A thin, bedraggled girl who looked about twelve, clad in shabby jeans and a bomber jacket, which offered little protection against the Canadian winter, stood shivering in the entrance.

"Thea! Come in. You look frozen." Victoria hauled the now-weeping girl into her arms and drew her into the kitchen. "Where have you been, honey? We've been worried sick."

Ben closed the door, put on the kettle and then left to find one of Tillie's afghans while Victoria grabbed a towel and briskly rubbed the half-frozen waif. Relief and irritation vied for supremacy.

Thea poured out the story of her journey as she shook off her coat and thin boots. Victoria swathed her in the afghan before phoning the social worker and Thea's sisters. That done, she sat down in front of her, held out a brimming mug of hot cocoa and began to speak.

"What were you thinking, Thea? You can't just up and run away when life gets tough." Suddenly aware that was exactly what she'd done, Victoria glanced sideways at Ben, who simply smiled encouragement. Relieved, Victoria continued to gently remonstrate with the young girl. "Everyone has been so worried about you, especially your foster family. You made them frantic."

"I d-didn't know you were so far away. I didn't think it would be so hard to get here." Between sobs and shivers, Thea told of her long trip to The Haven and the reason behind her sudden flight.

"You put us through this, worrying you were hurt or injured, or worse, because someone made fun of your jeans?" Victoria asked in disbelief, trying not to sound too harsh. "But, sweetheart, haters are everywhere. You can't always run away."

Ben edged toward the door, probably to give them some privacy, but Victoria needed him here, to support her.

"Don't go, Ben. I should have introduced you. This is Thea, one of my Little Sisters. The one we went searching for," she added with emphasis. "Thea, this is Ben."

"Hi." She nodded at Ben. "I knew it was a mistake as soon as I left the city, but I figured I'd look stupid going back so soon," she muttered.

"It's never stupid to admit you made a mistake, Thea. What is stupid is to keep on making it. Believe me, I know." She shared a look with Ben. "Ben and his nephew, Mikey, are staying at The Haven for a while. I'm sure Ben understands the urge to run."

"Huh?" Thea looked confused.

"Ben's a peacekeeper in Africa. I'd guess he gets lots of threats. Some of the people he's protecting probably don't think they need him there," Victoria explained. "But he doesn't run away no matter how hard it gets. He stands his ground."

Seeing Ben's appreciative smile made her realize she hadn't given enough thought to the difficulty of his job. She'd think more about that later, she decided, as he sat down and tried to look inconspicuous while Victoria refocused on her Little Sister.

"You're too smart to quit, Thea, and you have too much to offer to just give up and walk away because some dweeb at school made fun of you. But that's not really why you ran away, is it?" She leaned forward and grasped the girl's hands. "Tell me what's going on, honey."

"I want my family." Fresh tears burst from Thea. Her voice broke as she sobbed. "I want to be with my sisters, to have my own home. I want it to be the way it was."

"Oh, Thea." Victoria's heart broke as she enveloped the girl in her arms, offering comfort and an outlet for what had clearly been building for a while. "I know you do. But running away doesn't help. Deep in your heart you know that."

"But—"

"Sweetheart, your mom can't be the mother you want. At least not right now. She has to get herself straightened out." After a moment, Victoria eased Thea away and scooped her stringy hair out of her eyes. "I know you think nothing will ever be right again. But it will, if you're patient, if you look at what you have instead of what you don't. The Larsons love you, Thea. They're trying to help."

"They can't." Defiance filled the statement.

"Not if you won't let them." Victoria rubbed away the tears with her thumb. "Mrs. Larson isn't trying to replace your mother. She only wants to give you a comfortable, safe place to stay until your mom gets better."

"Why? What am I to her?" Thea demanded.

"A girl who, for a little while, needs a home." Victoria's soft response oozed love. "She's not trying to take anything. She's trying to *give* you something. Love."

"So I'll love her and forget about my mom."

Victoria caught Ben's smile at Thea's indignation.

"No!" she laughed, stemming her exasperation. "So you'll have a chance to become all you can be *in spite of* the problems in your family. Love isn't either-or, Thea. You can love more than one person. Otherwise you could only love one of your sisters."

"I guess," the girl said uncertainly.

"Loving Mrs. Larson doesn't take a thing away from the love you feel for your mom." Victoria spoke firmly. "You are not betraying your mother—you're showing that she raised you with a mature heart that can allow love to blossom and expand in your life, to enrich you and the people around you. But love can't grow when you're afraid."

Judging by Thea's frown, she wasn't buying everything she heard. But Victoria wasn't giving up. This was too important.

"We'll have supper in an hour or so, but I'm guessing you're hungry now?" Thea's strong affirmative response made her chuckle. "There's a bowl of leftover soup in the fridge. I'll heat that for you."

Just as Thea finished her soup the aunts returned with Mikey in tow. After introductions, the smiling seniors embraced Thea, warmly welcoming her to The Haven. While Mikey was telling Thea and Ben about his afternoon with his new friend, Garnet, Aunt Margaret cornered Victoria.

"How long will Thea be staying?"

"Not sure, Auntie. Her caseworker will probably get her as soon as she can." Victoria's troubled gaze rested on the girl. "Poor girl. She's stuck on how her family was and on getting that back."

"Is that likely to happen?" Margaret studied Victoria with an inscrutable expression.

"I'd say very unlikely after speaking to her social worker." Victoria touched her aunt's arm, her eyes pleading. "I want to spend as much time as I can with her, Auntie. Maybe if we talk long enough, she'll start to see that she needs to look ahead, not back."

"Take all the time you need, dear." Margaret's eyes sparkled. "Looking ahead is good advice for all of us." She noticed Ben watching them and chuckled. "You think Tillie and I are too old to look ahead very far, don't you, son?"

"Not at all." Ben's cheeks darkened telling Victoria that's exactly what he'd thought.

"Old age is a funny thing. You don't feel any differently than you did at twenty, except for the creaking joints." She mimed a wince as she bent her elbow. "But perspective changes with age. The older I get, the less life is about me. Now I'm focused on the future and the shape I'll leave the world for those who follow me."

"Old age is having a light shine on issues you didn't give much thought to before," Tillie agreed, joining the conversation. "You try to follow God's directions in hopes you can facilitate bringing the next generations closer to Him."

"I understand." Ben studied the pair. "You've determined that a refuge for foster kids can help do that so you're trying to create it."

"How could it be easier to get in touch with God than here in the glory of His creation?" Tilly wondered.

"All it takes is a leader." Margaret studied Victoria. "And we have a very capable one right here."

"Whoa, Aunties." Victoria frowned. "This isn't a done deal. We've got a long way to go to bring your imaginations to life."

"You've already accomplished more than we ever thought possible." Margaret's gaze swerved to Thea, who was laughing at Mikey's story about his friend. "And I believe God just sent us a test subject."

Victoria blinked, turned to look at Thea and then at her aunts. Finally her gaze rested on Ben. "You think?" she whispered.

"We all think," Tillie answered for everyone.

"The Lord works in mysterious ways," Margaret added. "We gave Him The Haven years ago and He keeps bringing seeking souls to us."

Victoria smiled at Ben, seeing his amusement at being called a seeking soul. But then, in some ways, so was she.

Only problem was, Victoria wasn't exactly sure what she was seeking—forgiveness, a future? Love?

That last one made her rush to prepare supper. She didn't want to consider love, and the future was still a mystery, especially to the aunts who didn't yet know about her baby.

But Ben had been a good friend whom she'd needed. The problem was, Victoria couldn't keep needing him because sooner or later, Ben was leaving.

And then she'd be a mother, on her own.

Chapter Seven

"It seems Thea's here for the weekend, at least until her social worker can get away to fetch her," Victoria murmured after closing her phone. She stared at Ben. "What are you doing?"

"Mending." Ben glanced up from weaving the needle and yarn through the heel of his sock and grinned at her. "Don't look so surprised. Mending's not rocket science."

"It is to me." Victoria's expression of distaste made him chuckle. "When my socks get holes, I chuck 'em."

"Not so easy to get socks like this in Africa. These are the best to wear with combat boots, but they're pricey." He paused to tie off his yarn before reminding her, "I'm trying to save every penny for the computer business I hope to open one day."

"Speaking of computers—you saw that?" Victoria inclined her head toward the fridge where Margaret had left a scrawled message attached by a magnet.

"That the seniors' center is having trouble with their computer—again? Yes." What Ben couldn't see was a trace of color in Victoria's cheeks. How long did morning sickness last, anyway? He needed to get a book on the subject and bone up on the issues Victoria would face so he'd know how to help.

"And?" Victoria's impatient voice drew him back to reality.

"I thought I'd check it out after my doctor's appointment." Ben was relieved that at least she was sipping a glass of orange juice. "*If* I can catch a ride into town with whomever is taking Mikey to story time at the library."

"I'll take you. I'm doing the reading." She ruffled the little boy's hair and laughed at his uncle's surprise. "You don't think I can read, Ben?" she teased.

"I thought you'd be up to your neck with stuff here." He lowered his voice. "Victoria, you look tired. Are you sure you're not taking on too much?"

"Reading a story to little kids is not work." She ignored his raised eyebrows and finished her juice. "If it makes you feel better, Thea is coming along. She's researching an assignment for school about story time. She'll help *if* I need it." Her tone clearly said she wouldn't.

Ben searched her face once more. But noting the resolution in her gray eyes, he gave up arguing. Instead he sat beside her on the window seat and pursued a different subject.

"Your aunts are entertaining a couple of 'guests' today," he said in a lowered voice. "So maybe it's a good thing we'll be out of the way."

"Another couple. Do you know anything about them?" Victoria's curiosity made her gray eyes darken.

"Tillie only said this couple has been wanting to adopt for a while. Which has me worried," he admitted.

"Why?" Victoria shot him a quizzical look before reaching for a stack of papers. She slid them into a turquoise leather pouch, which she then laid on a corner of the kitchen counter. "I thought you wanted parents for—" Her head tilted toward Mikey.

"I do," he assured her quickly. "But the way your aunts talk about this couple makes them sound older."

"So?" Victoria shrugged. "Older couples are often more established, more likely to have the resources to travel, which is," she reminded, "what you said you wanted."

"Yes, but I wasn't thinking of four-star hotel

kind of travel." Immediately a picture filled Ben's mind. "Will an older couple want to camp out under the stars to see the northern lights? Or go canoeing? Or be willing to fight mosquitoes in the woods to see God's amazing creatures up close and personal?"

Funny how each of the scenarios he pictured included Victoria.

"Ben." Her gently chiding voice did funny things to his breathing. "I think you're setting yourself and my aunts up for failure if you're expecting these couples to parent exactly as you would." Her glance trailed to Mikey who was racing cars across the tabletop, oblivious to them.

"I don't expect to parent at all."

"Ever?" She frowned. "I thought it was only Mikey—you *never* want to marry or have your own children?"

"I don't think I'm equipped for that responsibility."

"But what about the love of a family?" Victoria's troubled tone mirrored her solemn questions. "To have someone special in your world? To be that person in theirs? Are you willing to let your fear of responsibility cheat you out of the gift of love?"

"It's not fear," he informed her as he clenched his jaw.

But as they rode into town half an hour later,

Ben knew that was a lie. He was desperately afraid of love, afraid it would overpower him, put him into a situation that would mean relinquishing the control he'd clung to for years, control he'd used to keep his world on an even track.

Love for Neil and the utter helplessness of not being able to help him, to save him from the horror he'd gone through and the aftermath his brother had suffered getting out of his negative lifestyle remained a hard lump of guilt in Ben's gut. He hadn't done enough—should have done more.

Now he had to do the best thing he could for Mikey. Though he loved the boy dearly, he couldn't give in to those dreamy possibilities that tantalized him in the stillness of the night. He dared not let himself believe he could be Mikey's parent because he couldn't risk failing Mikey as he had Neil. As he had Issa.

"What about you, Victoria?" Ben asked when they'd entered the Chokecherry Hollow library, after Mikey dragged Thea off to meet his friend, Garnet. "Don't you want to fall in love, get married?"

"Once, that was all I wanted." Her face grew wistful as she murmured, "A husband who loved me, my own family to cherish—that was my heart's fondest wish."

"It isn't now?" he asked, following when she

shook off her bemusement and walked toward the big, comfy chair where she'd sit to read.

"Now it's time to grow up and face reality, Ben." Her tone was firm and, for Victoria, a bit cold. "I threw away my chance to have that dream."

"So have another dream. You're young. You'll meet…" He stopped, suddenly inexplicably uncomfortable with the idea of Victoria finding love. Which was silly because he wanted her to be happy.

"What man is going to take on someone else's child, Ben?" A tight smile lifted her lips. "Even if there was such a person, I don't have the time or the inclination to look for him. I've got my hands full with the aunts' project and having this baby. Prince Charming will have to take a back seat because my aunts and my baby come first."

As Victoria busied herself preparing, Ben glanced at the clock. His doctor's appointment was in five minutes. After promising to return to the library when he was finished, he walked to the medical clinic, where he received a clean bill of health from the doctor. Ben exited the office with a light heart. Now he could really help Jake around The Haven and maybe earn some of his keep before he left.

He was deep in thought about that and Victoria's ideas for the aunts' dream when a window display in one of the shops caught his eye. A long robe the color of expensive pearls hung invisibly supported, looking as if it had been spun out of silk. Immediately Ben envisioned Victoria wearing it, children gathered around her skirt while she gazed adoringly at their father, a faceless man with a build much like his own. His brain skittered away from that.

Neil had told him Alice loved it during her pregnancy when he'd bought her gifts, that they made her feel pretty when she didn't think she was. Who, Ben wondered, would buy Victoria special things? Who would be there to tell her she was pretty when pregnancy overwhelmed her?

It couldn't be him. He'd be gone in six weeks or so. Besides, Victoria had her aunts and her foster sisters to support her. She didn't need him. Ben told himself to walk on.

But he couldn't stop staring at the beautiful robe. A nearby church chimed the hour and he realized he should be at the library. And yet…

Ben walked inside the shop, pointed to the garment and asked about it.

"It's a bit costly," the salesperson explained. "That's because it's hand-crocheted."

Ben gulped when she told him the price. But how did you put a value on the welcome Victoria had given him, the love she kept showering on Mikey? How could a robe ever repay her for her generosity?

"I'll take it. And that book about pregnancy," he said.

Ben walked out of the store feeling a little embarrassed by the maternity-labeled bag, but glad he'd bought both the robe and the book. A sign reminding that Valentine's Day wasn't far off made him enter the next store and buy two pounds of fudge, maple-walnut for Tillie and bittersweet chocolate for Margaret. And he bought a chocolate car for Mikey. He'd give Victoria the wooden box he'd made for Valentine's Day.

The fudge store gave him a big bag to put everything inside, hiding the maternity-labeled bag. When Ben arrived at the library, Victoria was chatting with a group of moms and Thea was entertaining a toddler. Since Mikey and his friend were playing with paper airplanes Victoria had taught them to build during her story, Ben sat down to wait. His gaze automatically rested on Victoria.

"He's such a sweetie," she said, face glowing as she grazed her forefinger against the cheek of a newborn cradled in his mother's arms. "How are *you* doing?"

"I'm dead-tired all the time," the new mom responded with a sigh. "It's a struggle to even shower some mornings. But Terry's been great at taking over."

"It must be hard, Darla. But a friend of mine said something that might help you. She said she got through the tough times by remembering that it wouldn't last forever, and that one day she'd wish she could hold that baby again." Victoria bent and pressed a kiss to the infant's cheek. "Realizing that helped her treasure the moments even when she was dead-tired."

"Good advice. It seems like just last week that I was going through this with Garnet and now he's so busy. Sometimes I wish I could hold him for a moment longer, but he wriggles away." Both women turned to watch Mikey and Garnet with fond smiles.

Then Victoria noticed Ben. She nodded at him, excused herself and called to Thea. Within minutes, the two had packed up their supplies. Having just overheard how tired Garnet's mom was, Ben had an idea.

"Would it be okay to invite Garnet to play at The Haven with Mikey one afternoon?" he asked Victoria. "Maybe it would give his mom a break. I didn't realize she had a new baby."

"That's kind of you. I think Darla would appreciate that."

Her smile was enough to chase away all Ben's doubts about buying the robe for her. He wasn't sure when he'd give it to her, but he was pretty sure she'd like it.

With everything packed, she turned to him. "What did the doctor say?"

"I'm good as new," he reported. "It's going to be a bit of a wait for you while I'm at the seniors' center though. I saw a ton of cars in their parking lot."

"Could we have lunch in town and then go skating while you do your computer thing?" Thea suggested before high-fiving a grinning Mikey.

"You don't have skates." Ben studied Victoria, trying to find a way to say he didn't think she should be skating and knowing he didn't have the right to offer her that advice.

"Maybe we can rent them?" Thea looked at Victoria whose face had grown pensive as she studied her Little Sister.

"You still like skating, huh, Thea?" Victoria seemed surprised.

"I know you thought I'd grow out of it, but ever since you took us skating last year, I've been addicted." Thea glibly listed the current reigning Canadian male and female figure skaters. "I'm saving up to buy a new pair of skates so I can skate like them. My feet are too big for the ones you bought me at that yard sale last year, Vic." Her eyes widened. "Hey! Too bad you couldn't make a skating rink at The Haven. I'd love to skate outdoors."

"It's an idea." Victoria met Ben's glance with a secretive smile then said, "So, lunch in town, Major. What are you thinking?"

"Burgers. Big, fat, juicy ones," he said. "Or not," he immediately backtracked because the expression on her face made him think burgers probably weren't the healthiest choice for kids.

"Burgers it is," Victoria agreed before he could change his mind. "There's a place across the street that makes their own. Want to try it?"

"It's up to you," Ben told her.

"I'm good with that." She smiled, but something hid behind the faint tilt of her lips that he didn't understand.

"If we're going skating after lunch, why don't we ask if Garnet can come with us for lunch and then skating?" Thea asked.

"You're such a clever girl." Victoria hugged her briefly, her face soft with love. Then she hurried to stop the departing mom. Darla grinned before nodding at Garnet who raced toward Mikey. Victoria followed. "All set, everyone?"

Outside, they waited for the village traffic to allow them to cross the street, the two boys in front with Thea who'd apparently decided to play babysitter.

"We don't have to eat hamburgers if you'd rather not," Ben said quietly.

"It's fine." Victoria glanced down the street and frowned. "Oh. It's gone."

"What is?" He studied the building in front of him. "Little Joe's Burgers? The sign says it's open. Or isn't this the place you meant?"

"There was a robe on display—" Her smile seemed forced. "Never mind."

Ben held the door then followed them to a table. The aroma of frying onions made his stomach growl. By contrast, Victoria held one glove over her nose as she slid into a booth across from Thea, Garnet and Mikey.

"Okay?" he asked while Thea explained the menu to the two boys.

"Yes." Victoria's response didn't reassure him and he guessed his face showed it because she admitted, "Sometimes certain smells like frying onions make me a bit queasy. I'll be fine."

But the way she grabbed the water glass their server delivered and swallowed half of it belied her comment. He ordered his burger without onions to spare her. Mikey's burger was plain like Garnet's, and Thea wanted soup.

"I love soup," she said, closing her eyes in what Ben was coming to recognize her naturally dramatic tone.

Victoria's order made Ben blink.

"Can I have half a cantaloupe?" When the server nodded, she grinned. "With a scoop of ice cream, toast and peanut butter and a dill pickle?"

Talk about queasy. But the server nodded and departed as if used to such unusual requests.

"Interesting combination," Ben murmured while the two boys listened to Thea's explanation about figure skater's clothes.

"Goofy, I know." Victoria shrugged. "But that's what I'm craving. I think it comes with the territory." She patted her stomach.

"So how else can I help with this dinner next Thursday?" Ben couldn't fathom how a dining room, even one as large as The Haven's would hold forty.

"Party meals at The Haven work best in the dining room because that table extends to ten feet. People can work their way around it, choose their food and mingle as they eat," Victoria explained, her enthusiasm obvious.

"What about chairs?" he wondered. Or did they eat standing up?

"The aunts bought a bunch of collapsible chairs eons ago when they were holding Bible studies at The Haven. They're stored in one of the garages," she said in an airy tone that showed no stress about hosting so many people. "If you and Jake bring those in on Wednesday, we could clean them up and set them around. I'll order a couple of table arrangements and choose some music and that's about it."

"You make it sound simple to feed such a large group." Ben blinked.

"The hard work is the menu and Adele's an expert at that. The rest isn't rocket science. We've done it many times." Victoria chuckled. "When we moved here, we girls soon learned that Aunt Tillie and Margaret love any excuse for a party."

But forty people? Ben couldn't quite believe she was so calm.

"The youth group will serve punch and hot drinks. They'll also clear up the dishes." Victoria chuckled at his expression. "They love to do it. My aunts pay them and they use the money for youth group excursions. Their last one was a weekend trip to the water park at the West Edmonton Mall before Christmas. They presented a slideshow about it at church and it was hilarious."

"I don't have to be at the dinner though, right?" Ben asked diffidently. "I mean, I'm not part of your family or community..." Odd how left out that made him feel.

"Of course you must be at our party," Victoria insisted. "The aunts have been talking you up nonstop. Everyone wants to meet our UN peacekeeper."

"Oh." Ben was glad their food arrived, because

now *he* was nervous about Thursday. "Well, if I can help, just ask."

While the males dug into their burgers and Thea raved about her soup, Victoria carefully spread a lavish amount of peanut butter on her toast, added circles of pickle on top and took tiny bites of it, alternating with the melon.

"How is it?" he asked curiously.

"Excellent. Want to try?" Victoria held out a piece of toast, shrugged when he declined then popped it into her mouth. "So good," she said with a rapt expression.

"I've heard pickles are a favorite of ladies—" Suddenly aware of Thea's attention, he clipped off the rest of his comment.

"Vic always eats peanut butter and dill pickles. She keeps a couple of extra jars of both at her place so she doesn't run out." Thea made a face. "My sisters and I tried it once. It wasn't our favorite."

"More for me." Undeterred, Victoria finished her lunch then asked for hot tea.

"Can I have some, too?" Thea asked and added, "Please?" when the server wisely looked at Victoria for permission.

"Since it's herbal and decaf, yes. You're too young for caffeine." The words were firm but there was a gentle, loving sound in them that revealed Victoria's fondness for Thea.

Ben considered the way she dealt with the children. She didn't seem to doubt her decisions or second-guess her choices. Nothing seemed to overwhelm Victoria. She handled the obstacles that came along in her life with a serenity he envied. He would never feel such poise and confidence if he took on parenting Mikey. Every single decision seemed rife with the possibility of failure.

But then Victoria hadn't made the mistakes he had.

Chilly and tired after two hours of supervising skating, Victoria sat in a corner of the seniors' center, intrigued by the sight of quiet, reserved Ben in the role of teacher. A tiny smile curved her lips as he patiently explained, for the third time, how to import pictures from a camera chip.

Sprawled in a chair beside her, Thea appeared totally engrossed in a skating magazine that Victoria had purchased at the local drugstore. Mikey and Garnet were quietly playing nearby with the dinky cars she'd bought at the same time. That left Victoria free to watch Ben; as if she could help it.

He was like no man Victoria had ever known. The seniors held his complete attention. He didn't seem to care how long it took him; he patiently made sure whoever needed him received help.

Nor did he appear to mind when one of the elderly ladies accidentally spilled her coffee on his shirt, or that the hard-of-hearing gent to his left kept asking him to repeat everything. Ben was on a mission to make sure every single attendee would be able to get their photos in an album on the computer and nothing was going to stop him.

Wouldn't it be amazing to have someone like that, someone so confident, assured and willing to do what was needed—wouldn't it be wonderful to have Ben in her world all the time?

Silly. She couldn't think that way. Ben wasn't staying. And anyway, he didn't feel he could handle Mikey in his life full-time. How could he possibly deal with a new baby? If only…

Victoria's gaze traveled to Mikey and rested on his happy face, his wide grin. She noticed the way he engaged with Garnet. This Mikey was a far cry from the withdrawn little boy who'd arrived at The Haven during the first week of January, scared of the dogs and the dark. He still mentioned his parents, but mostly with happy memories. There were fewer tearful moments. But Ben's imminent departure and how that would affect this sweet child worried her. Somehow she had to help Ben realize he was capable of fathering.

Victoria's ringing phone interrupted her thoughts. She moved to a quieter corner as she listened to Thea's social worker explain in hurried detail why she wouldn't be able to pick up the girl over the weekend as they'd discussed last night.

"I'm so sorry. Naturally you can't leave in the middle of such a situation. Too bad her foster mom's down with the flu." She deliberately kept her back to Thea. "What can I do to help?"

The response was unsettling and there was little time to mull it over because Ben finished up his class and joined her.

"I'll think about it and let you know tonight," she promised before hanging up.

"Something wrong?" he asked as they walked out to the car. "Did Mikey cause a problem?"

"No, skating was great." Victoria forced away her concern as they dropped off Garnet and during the drive home.

Since the aunts had dinner ready to serve and the children were full of stories in between bites, there was no need for Victoria to make conversation. Once the kitchen was cleaned up, Ben left to put Mikey to bed. When Thea went to her room, as well, Victoria informed Tillie and Margaret of her phone call.

"Will the girl go to school here, then?" Margaret asked worriedly. "She's already missed several days."

"Elaine, her social worker, asked if I could take Thea to Edmonton," Victoria explained. "It might be a good idea. Since I don't intend to return there in the immediate future, I could use this trip to vacate my apartment."

"You're staying here? For good?" Tillie clasped her hands together, her eyes glossy with tears. "How wonderful!"

"It surely is. But, my dear, how can you make such a long trip let alone pack up when you're still feeling poorly? And our dinner is next week." Margaret's frown told Victoria she was considering all the angles.

"I'll manage," she responded, ducking her head as her cheeks burned with shame. Sooner or later, she was going to have to tell them about the baby. "I actually don't have tons to move. I'd planned to replace my old college furniture anyway so I'll donate it to charity." She couldn't sit still any longer. "I'm going for a walk to think through everything."

"Take a flashlight, dear." The aunts were used to her walks. They understood she needed space to wrap her mind around a problem.

Outside, the full moon reflected off the snow like a massive streetlight. With no wind, the grounds were eerily silent. Only the sound of her footsteps crunching through the crusted snow echoed back to her. Victoria walked all the way down the driveway and back. Finally tired yet still without answers, she brushed the snow off the cement table on the patio and sat down.

"I know I have to tell them, God." Victoria cringed at the hurt she knew she'd see on her aunts' precious faces. But she couldn't stay here with them and keep living a lie, pretending nothing had changed.

"Are you all right?" The low rumble of Ben's voice was like a comforting blanket. His hip nudged hers as he sat beside her. "What are you doing out here, Victoria?"

"Trying to figure a way out of the hole I've dug for myself," she muttered.

"You're making too much of it. Your aunts love you." Funny how he immediately understood her battle. "They'll be delighted to embrace you and your baby."

"How do you know that, Ben?" she whispered. "How can you be so certain? You barely know them."

"I know you. I know your heart," he answered calmly. "I know they helped shape you into the woman you've become. Thoughtful, kind, generous, considerate. You love them and they love you."

"But is love enough?"

"That's funny coming from you." When she looked at him, he was smiling. "Aren't you the one who believes love conquers everything?" He grabbed her gloved hand and wrapped his own around it, his expression earnest. "When Thea made a mistake and ran away, how did you feel?"

"Sorry that she made that mistake," Victoria said while thinking how handsome he was. "Sorry for the pain it caused her, that she had to go through it."

"You don't love her any less?" He kept his gaze on her face, watching her reaction. "You aren't ashamed of her or embarrassed that she made that mistake?"

"Of course not." Victoria didn't try to mask her indignation. "Everyone makes mistakes. She's my Little Sister and I love her. That won't change."

"Exactly," he said, his grin stretching wide. "So why would you even imagine that your aunts are going to feel differently about you when they learn you made a mistake?"

"The consequences are a little more severe in my case, Ben," she said in a droll tone.

He was silent for a long time. That was okay with Victoria—it gave her time to think. But clarity was hard to find with him sitting so near, holding her hand.

"When Neil got married, I was his best man. He was terrified he was going to forget the old-fashioned vows he and Alice had chosen," he said, a hint of loss in the quiet words.

Victoria squeezed his hand for comfort, unsure of what he was leading up to.

"It's funny how I keep remembering those words. *For better or worse, richer or poorer, in sickness and in health. So long as we both shall live.* That's the promise they made to each other." Ben shifted so he could look fully into her face. "I think those words say exactly what love really means—that you'll be there for the other person no matter what mistakes they make. Right?"

"Exactly right, Ben," Victoria whispered past the lump in her throat. What a man. Why hadn't she met him first?

"The more I learn about God, the more I understand that's exactly the kind of love He offers us. Unconditional." Noting her shiver, Ben slid his arm around her waist and drew her close to his side. "Tell your aunts, Victoria," he said very quietly, his warm breath brushing her ear. "Tell them and let yourself off the hook."

"When?"

"As soon as possible."

It felt so right to stay there, to lay her head on his shoulder and watch the northern lights dance. She'd sat here a hundred times before, seen the sky blaze and flare so often, but not once had she felt this intense connection with someone, as if this was where she belonged. And Ben was part of it.

But Ben was leaving.

"I'll tell them tonight," she said with a sigh, then added, "I need you to pray, Ben." An idea sprang. "Would you also be there with me?"

"This is private, between you and your aunts," he protested. "I'm the outsider."

"No." Victoria hated to leave the sweet comfort he offered but she rose, dusted off the snow and faced him. "This is your home now, Ben. You're a part of our family. Please, will you be there, help me face them?"

He studied her for a long time, his face a mask hiding his thoughts. Finally he gave a nod.

"If you want me to, I'll be there," he said. "Praying."

"Thank you, Ben. Thank you very much." Relieved, Victoria started walking toward The Haven's back door, comforted that he was at her side.

But as they shed their coats and went to find Tillie and Margaret, a little voice inside Victoria's head chanted, *Don't get used to it, girl. Ben's not going to be here every time you need him.*

With firm deliberation, she shut off the voice and faced the two women who'd loved her through everything the past fifteen years had brought.

"Aunties," she said, sinking onto the hearth, in front of the family room's roaring fire. "I need to tell you something."

Chapter Eight

Ben's heart ached for Victoria. Her face was paler than he'd ever seen it as she tearfully confessed to her aunts.

"I'm so sorry. I know you taught me better than that. I know you'll be embarrassed and ashamed when I get as big as a house," she spluttered, the tears freely tumbling down her cheeks. "Maybe you won't even want me here. I won't be much of an example to the foster kids."

"A baby." Tillie couldn't seem to get past that. Her eyes glowed with excitement as she stared into the fire. "A baby at The Haven."

"I wondered how long you'd wait to tell us." Margaret's face had softened, too. "I guessed the truth some time ago, Victoria. I'm just sorry you felt you had to keep it from us. We love you, dear. No matter what. Don't you understand that?"

"But—"

Margaret held up a hand for silence.

"Have you asked God for forgiveness?" Her face stern, she waited for Victoria's nod.

"A thousand times, Auntie." Victoria scrubbed the tears from her face.

"Why a thousand times?" Tillie asked. "Our Father is gracious and forgiving. He doesn't need you to beg Him. From the moment you asked, He put it in the past, to be remembered no more."

"I know but—"

"That doesn't mean there won't be issues and hardships to deal with," Margaret said bluntly. "But we shall deal with them together. As we always have."

"Yes." Tillie grinned at her sister. "But we've never had a baby at The Haven before."

Ben remained silent as the three embraced and then began chatting about all things baby. Once more, he felt outside the circle, a mere spectator. But that was only for a moment.

"Ben guessed, too," Victoria said and tossed a smile at him. "He's been urging me to tell you."

"Major Ben has a good head on his shoulders." Tillie rose to hug him then mused, "I'll need to knit the baby a blanket. What color, I wonder?"

"You're bound to get tired, Victoria. Are you sure these changes for The Haven are doable for you?" Margaret studied her with a frown. "We don't want you ill or run down."

"It will be a challenge," Victoria agreed. "But I can get help from you and Jake and my sisters. And Ben will help...while he's here." She added on the last part almost as an afterthought.

"I'll gladly do whatever I can," he agreed while wondering if Victoria had been reminding him that he wasn't staying here forever, despite her insistence that The Haven was his home.

"We'll take it one step at a time," Margaret said firmly. "After all, this is the Lord's project and He knows all about what we'll face."

"I know it's Valentine's Day tomorrow but I've decided to take Thea to Edmonton. While I'm there, I'll pack up my stuff. I'm moving home to The Haven again, Aunties." Her grin was huge when the ladies cheered.

"Mikey and I will go with you, if you don't mind, Victoria." Ben smiled at her surprise. "I want to see the insurance people and there are several estate matters I need to deal with."

"Are you sure you're not coming just to make sure I don't change my mind about staying?" she teased.

"Maybe." For some reason, the thought of Victoria seeing her former boyfriend irritated Ben, which was silly. "Mostly I'm coming to help with whatever needs doing."

"You're very sweet, Ben." She cupped his

cheek in her palm, her gray eyes softening with her smile. "Thank you."

"My pleasure."

Half an hour later, Ben excused himself so the three ladies could have some private time. But Victoria stopped him by wrapping her arms around him in a big hug.

"I can't tell you how much it helped to know you were there praying for me," she whispered when she finally drew away.

With his heart racing, Ben took a moment before responding. "I'm glad, but I knew it would go well. They love you, Victoria. They were never going to condemn you. How early do you want to start out tomorrow?"

She suggested a time. He bid everyone goodnight and went to his room. But sleep was elusive. Ben couldn't seem to stop comparing the risks Victoria was prepared to take to become a mother with the risks he was afraid to take with Mikey. Was he doing the right thing? Would he one day regret the time he hadn't spent with his nephew, the love he hadn't built on? Would he wish he'd at least tried to father Mikey, mistakes and all?

What's the right thing to do? he prayed silently. *Isn't it better for Mikey to have two parents than one bachelor uncle who doesn't know anything about raising a child?*

Ben picked up his phone and reread the message he'd received that morning.

Please confirm your intent to return to your post on April 10 as per earlier arrangements.

He needed to send his confirmation to his commanding officer who'd then notify command. But doubts about that response plagued him. Was it really more important to guard people in Africa than it was to ensure Neil's son was safe and happy?

Ben tried to clear his mind and force himself to relax. It would be enough to deal with his brother's affairs in Edmonton and to help Victoria. Hopefully he wouldn't have time to rethink his decision about Mikey. But he couldn't rest.

So Ben rose before dawn, showered and then spent time with his Bible and in prayer. At six, he snuck downstairs and laid out his Valentine's gifts and cards, made coffee. Then he hurried back to his room when he heard someone stirring. Ten minutes later, he woke Mikey to prepare him for the journey.

"Where we goin', Unca Ben?" Mikey climbed onto Ben's knee, buried his head against his chest and yawned.

"We're going on a trip." Ben inhaled the little-boy-freshly-woken scent of him, savoring the moment and his bond with this sweet child. "We're going with Victoria to Edmonton." He wasn't sure how much to say.

"That's where I live." Mikey sat up straight, his face puzzled. "Are we goin' to my old house to see Mommy and Daddy?"

"No, Mikey." Ben swallowed and spoke past the lump in his throat. "They're in Heaven, remember?" *Please don't make me go through this again*, he prayed silently.

"With God, right?" Mikey nestled against him again. "Are we going to see the place then?"

The place was Mikey-speak for the cemetery where his parents' graves were.

"We can, if you want to." Should he have said no, kept the boy away from that sad place? Or was it healthy for him to see the graves? The weight of these decisions was what bothered Ben. He never felt comfortable with his choices, always questioned his decisions.

"I could show Vic." Mikey yawned again. "It's still dark outside, Unca Ben."

"I know. It's really early. That's why we have to be quiet while we get ready."

"'Cause the aunties are still sleeping, right?" Mikey asked.

"Right." Ben smiled as he helped his nephew wash up, don warm pants, thick socks and a heavy sweater. He relished the sweet pleasure of Mikey's nonstop chatter. When it dawned on him that soon someone else would be in his place, watching this child grow and change through a host of mornings, a gush of sadness filled him.

"Are we having breakfast now?" Mikey asked after he'd helped make his bed.

"Yes. Quietly now as we go downstairs." He smothered his chuckle as Mikey tiptoed in an exaggerated fashion down each stair tread and then across the hardwood floor into the kitchen.

Mikey's silence was completely ruined by his shriek of joy at finding Victoria and Thea already in the kitchen examining the gifts.

"Happy Valentine's Day, everyone," Ben said as he entered.

Thea thanked him profusely for the new book on skating and Mikey for his chocolate car. Victoria praised him effusively for the box, complimenting his woodworking skill. Assured by her that Tillie and Margaret would love the fudge he'd left in their study, Ben poured himself coffee and sat down, wondering if he should have left the robe, too, yet somehow feeling it was more appropriate for a special occasion.

"Unca Ben tol' me we're goin' on a trip." Mikey frowned at the bowl Victoria set in front of him. "What's that?" His nose wrinkled and turned up.

"It's porridge, my most favorite thing to eat in the morning." She winked at Ben as she set a bowl for him, one for Thea and a smaller one for herself.

Ben was relieved that Victoria didn't look as pale as usual this morning. In fact, there was an air about her that said she was anticipating a return to the city. He sure hoped that glow didn't come from thoughts of meeting her former boyfriend, though he quickly forgot that when she sat down beside him and smiled, gray eyes sparkling.

"Happy Valentine's Day, Ben."

"And to you, Victoria."

Mikey had tasted the cereal and was not happy.

"C'n I have toast? Please." He tossed a worried sideways glance at Ben who had to choke back his amusement at the little boy's extreme politeness.

"Wait. You have to taste it with this. Like Thea is." Victoria poured maple syrup on top, added a pinch of cinnamon and some milk and then held out a spoon. "Try it now."

Mikey looked at Ben again with a look that clearly asked, *Do I have to?* Ben wasn't sure what to do. He figured he was supposed to encourage the kid so he'd have new experiences, but on the other hand, maybe forcing him would cause some psychological trauma. Confused, he remained silent.

"Try it, Mikey," Thea urged.

"Please?" Victoria softly pleaded. "If you don't like it, I promise I'll make you toast."

"With peanut butter? I really like peanut butter," Mikey informed her.

When she nodded, he slowly picked up his spoon and gingerly dipped it into the cereal. With an infinitesimal amount of porridge barely visible on the tip of the spoon, he inhaled deeply before pushing it a fraction of an inch into his mouth. A second later, his eyes widened and he took a second helping, a full spoonful this time.

"So?" Victoria asked, her grin peeking out.

"It's dee-lish," Mikey exclaimed.

Ben made a mental note. *Get him to taste without force.* How did Victoria know to do that? He put it down to her training to be a teacher, choosing to ignore his brain's reminder that she hadn't taught very long. Women were natural nurturers, he decided then winced.

"Nurturing doesn't have to do with whether you're a man or a woman," his sister-in-law, Alice, had once scolded him. *"It has to do with your heart, Ben, and whether or not you're willing to let it be open enough to consider others' needs before your own."*

Whatever it took to be a nurturer, Victoria certainly had it in spades. Ben watched her give handmade cards to the two children and he accepted Mikey's valentine. He admired Victoria's ease with Mikey and Thea as she teased and joked with them, but he was also a little jealous. If only he could relax like that instead of feeling so uptight and nervous about every decision related to Mikey.

Yet Ben was infinitely glad Victoria was there, showing him without words what skills a caregiver needed. If nothing else, learning from her ought to make him better able to judge the appropriate parents for Mikey.

When Thea took Mikey to wash his hands and face, Victoria set an envelope on the table. "This is for you."

"Thank you." Ben opened it slowly and found a handmade card with a Bible verse and careful printing that said, *Happy Valentine's Day. Glad you could share this day with us*. "I'm glad, too," he said, slightly amazed by how true that was. "You look better this morning, Victoria. No morning sickness?"

"Earlier." She made a face. "If I get up and get it over with, I can get on with my day."

He was going to ask how early she'd had to get up to do that but didn't because the children had returned. It took a few minutes to stow their bags in Victoria's SUV and say goodbye to newly awakened Tillie and Margaret who came into the kitchen in matching fuzzy pink robes, their hair twisted in exactly the same style around spongy pink rollers. As Ben returned their goodbye hugs, he wondered how they could sleep in such things.

"We made a good getaway timewise," Victoria said when they were finally moving down the road. Her voice dropped beneath the kids' chatter. "Thank you for offering to drive. I was wondering if..."

"You thought you'd feel carsick?" He hoped not. She looked beautifully vivacious in her bright red jacket.

"So far I feel fine so you can stop frowning," Victoria said with a laugh.

Ben loved hearing Victoria's laugh. It was such a joyous happy sound that made the world seem immediately brighter. It was like they were on a family trip. In the rearview mirror, he saw Thea was entranced by her magazine, but his nephew was hunched over. "How are you doing, Mikey?"

"Good. C'n I color people's hair blue, Vic?" he asked.

"Why not?" Victoria said gaily. "On a frosty, wintry morning like this, it feels like anything's possible."

As the sun rose over the mountain tops, Ben found no reason to disagree with her.

"Oh, look." She pointed toward a black gelding, standing next to a white rail fence. "Shade's still there."

"The horse? Why wouldn't he be?" Ben wondered as he took the right-hand turn that put them on the highway toward Edmonton.

"Because Shade is very old. He was my favorite horse all through high school. I loved that horse." Her face softened with memories. "When we get back, I need to go visit him."

"You rided a horse, Vic?" Mikey sounded amazed.

"Used to. All the time. It was my favorite thing." She paused then added, "I found a stable in the city where I could ride, but it became too expensive."

"She took my sisters and me riding once," Thea volunteered. "It was fun."

"Yes, it was. I wonder where my cowboy boots are." Victoria fell silent for a moment. Then she gasped.

"What's wrong?" Ben clenched his hands on the wheel. "Should I pull over? Do you feel sick?"

"I feel fine. And incredibly stupid." Her oval face grew alive with excitement. "I haven't been thinking straight, Ben."

"About?" She didn't look sick so he maintained his speed.

"About things for our kids to do when they come to The Haven."

Our kids? He felt his chest expand with pride at being included in Victoria's new goal.

"McDowell Stables is The Haven's nearest

neighbor," she explained. "In fact, there used to be a path worn from the stables to The Haven. I should know. I made it. What foster kid from the city wouldn't like to learn to ride a horse, Thea? Mikey?"

"Me," Mikey assured her.

"Me, too," Thea agreed.

"Good. We'll check into that when we get back," she promised with a giggle.

"Do I gotta get cowboy boots?" Mikey asked hopefully.

"We'll have to see," Ben temporized. At least he'd learned that much. Never promise what you might not be able to deliver.

"I went to school with Mac McDowell. He loved that ranch something fierce, wanted to run the spread, but his parents insisted he go to university first. I lost track of him. I wonder if he runs the ranch now. I'll have to ask the aunts." She peered ahead. "Mac was the best-looking guy in high school."

"You had a crush on him," Ben said, knowing it was true when her cheeks flushed a deep rose. The flower of jealousy bloomed inside. That kept happening lately. Which was silly because, though he really liked Victoria, he wasn't going to get involved with any woman. He was returning to Africa.

Forcing his mind off Victoria and on to the

things he hoped to accomplish while he was in the city kept Ben focused on driving. Victoria fell asleep, her glossy dark head resting on the seat back, long lush lashes against her pale cheeks. Mikey and Thea soon followed, their soft snores filling the car and leaving Ben alone with his thoughts.

First thing on his list was retrieving the personal items that had been in the trunk of his car when he'd wrecked it. He desperately wanted to go through Neil and Alice's papers before he left the country and ensure the important ones were safely stored for Mikey when he was old enough to see them. But his main goal was to help Victoria pack. No way was she going to overdo things on his watch.

Some inner secret part of Ben desperately hoped she didn't intend to get in touch with her former boyfriend. He didn't ask himself why the very thought of it irritated him. Victoria wasn't his. He had no right to censor whom she saw.

He wished he did.

"Victoria."

The sound of her own name ended a sweet dream where she and Ben had been together, sliding down a snow-covered hill at The Haven. She blinked awake to find her fingers were clenched as if she was still firmly gripping his waist and that she was grinning like a lovesick school girl.

"Good dream?" Ben asked when she glanced at him.

"Very good," she responded truthfully, a little embarrassed to admit how much she'd been enjoying it.

"Want to share?"

"No." She glanced out the window. "It was just a dream." And that was something she needed to stop doing by remembering Ben wasn't going to be part of her life in the long term.

"So what's first on the agenda, Victoria?"

"We need to get Thea home. Take the next exit." She directed him through a maze of streets to a lovely Tudor-style home on a pretty block, where the lawns of each house bore testament that many kids lived in this neighborhood. Snow forts, snowmen and sleds of all descriptions littered the white-covered lawns. "Thea, you're home," Victoria said firmly enough to waken the girl.

"Oh." Thea stretched then tucked her magazine into her backpack. "I suppose I'll be grounded now."

"Don't you think you should be?" Victoria twisted to face her, determined to ensure that Thea was prepared to accept the consequences for her actions. "Honey, what you did was foolhardy, dangerous and caused a lot of worry. You need to apologize."

"I know." Thea had phoned her foster parents before they left The Haven and now the couple rushed out of the house toward the car. She said thank you to Ben then climbed out and into the arms of her sobbing foster mom.

Victoria also exited the car, grateful that Ben stayed where he was. She didn't want to embarrass Thea in front of him, but she couldn't walk away without making sure Thea's parents would forgive her. She was happily relieved by their loving attitude and even more so that their foster daughter finally seemed willing to accept that they loved her.

Her heart breaking, Victoria faced this girl she loved so dearly.

"I've already explained why I can't be your Big Sister anymore, Thea. But I will always be your friend who loves you and your sisters and cares about you. You can text me or call me anytime and I'll love to hear from you. When I come to Edmonton, we'll go for lunch, if your foster mom says it's okay."

"I'd like that." Thea had her brave face on.

"Please, Thea," she whispered. "Please open your heart to love. Your foster mom and dad are good people, and they care about you deeply. Before you decide to do anything like this again, stop and think. Don't shut them out. Talk to them. Let them love you. I promise it will make your life so much happier."

"I'll try. Thank you, Victoria." Openly crying, Thea enveloped her in a tight embrace. "I hope I can come see you at The Haven sometime."

"We'll try to make that happen. But for now, you're loved here, sweetie. Don't push that away." Then Victoria eased free, said goodbye to Thea's foster parents and climbed back inside the car.

"Are you cryin', Vic?" Mikey asked in awe.

"Yes." She dashed away her tears as she smiled at him.

"How come?"

Victoria was choked up, but she had to explain to this boy who would soon lose his uncle. "It hurts to let go of someone you love, Mikey."

"'Cause you like bein' her Big Sister, right?" The four-year-old waited for her to nod. "So why can't you be that no more?"

"That's not what's best for Thea, Mikey." Victoria blew her nose then turned to face him. "I love Thea. But she needs a different Big Sister who lives in Edmonton, someone who can come running when she needs them. I can't do that anymore."

"That hurts you." One chubby finger reached out to brush her cheek.

"Sometimes loving people does hurt," Victoria

explained gently. She lifted her head. Her eyes met Ben's. "Especially when you have to let go."

Did he fully comprehend what giving this precious child into someone else's care would cost him? When Ben was standing guard over other children, other families in that barren African post, would he wish he'd stayed, braved his worries and spent the precious moments of Mikey's childhood watching over *him*?

It isn't right, Lord. Can't You help?

"Victoria?" Ben's voice drew her from her prayer. "Where do I drive next?"

Help me show him what he will miss out on, God. Today and tomorrow let him find courage in Your strength.

"Victoria?" Ben's hand rested on her arm, drawing her gaze to his. "Everything okay?"

"Yes," she said as hope and faith comingled in a bubble of excitement. "I just thought of a verse I memorized a long time ago, something that makes letting go of Thea easier. 'In all your ways acknowledge Him and He will direct your paths.' Maybe if I hang on to that, I'll grow more comfortable with trusting God for the next step in my life."

"And the next step is emptying your place. So where to?" Ben asked, one dark eyebrow arched.

"Left at the corner, please." She leaned back in her seat, her brain whirling.

Ben feared responsibility. Maybe if she was strong enough, he'd realize God had given him everything he needed to do the job of fathering Mikey.

Chapter Nine

Ben hated Victoria's place. It was nothing like her. In no way did it express her generous, happy personality. He especially didn't like her intention to stay here overnight while he and Mikey camped at a comfortable hotel.

"The Goodwill truck is coming for the sofa and dinette in half an hour. Why not send the bed along?" he suggested late in the afternoon when her weariness was obvious. "It would be easier than trying to get them to come back later and a lot simpler to clean the place if it was out of the way."

"But I was going to sleep here," she said with a frown.

"You can stay at the same hotel Mikey and I will be at." Ben could see her objections mounting but he held firm. "Come on, Victoria. This is a lot of work. You said you had a doctor's appointment tomorrow. You need your rest. One night at a hotel room is worth it." Her jaw thrust up in the manner that he knew meant she'd argue so he quickly added, "Why do you want to stay here anyway? It's an ugly place."

"It is, isn't it?" She glanced around as if she'd never really seen it clearly. "I had so many plans when I moved in here. I was going to paint, get new furniture, have that patio door fixed."

"Your landlord should have done that." He added the box Mikey had filled to the growing stack by the door. "Good job, kid."

"Thanks, Unca Ben." Mikey's grin gleamed white from his dusty face. "I put all the popsicle sticks together, an' all the white balls, an' all the glue bottles. There sure are a lot of things, but I got 'em in," he added proudly.

"You did great, Mikey." Victoria hugged him. "Thank you for helping with all those craft things. I was going to use them with my Little Sisters someday, but—" she sighed and sniffed.

"The kids at that day care place will like 'em, Vic," Mikey assured her. "Unca Ben said they mostly don't get nice stuff."

"No, they don't. They try to keep costs low." She sank onto what Ben had learned was her favorite chair though why he couldn't imagine. He'd sat in it earlier and still felt pain from the loose spring.

"I'm glad you agreed to send those craft things there." He tried to hide his relief that he didn't have to cart all that musty-smelling stuff to the car and then into The Haven. "Where'd you get it all?"

"Auction sale. Nobody bid on it so I got it for a song."

Ben figured the smell of items kept in dank storage had probably kept other buyers to a minimum. Victoria suddenly sat up straight.

"Maybe we should keep it for kids who come to The Haven?"

"I thought the idea was to get the kids outdoors." He maintained his blank expression with difficulty. "Besides, you've already promised the day care."

"True." She leaned back, resting her head against the chair as she looked around. "I traveled so much and my Little Sisters kept me so busy that I was seldom here. I didn't notice what a sad little place this is and how shabby everything has become."

"You deserve better," he said quietly.

"I wonder when I became so satisfied with making do?" she murmured, her gaze introspective.

Ben said nothing. She looked weary, though her face brightened when Mikey snuggled onto her knee. The two shared a glance of perfect harmony that made his heart ache until the door buzzer sounded.

"That must be the Goodwill folks." Relieved that Victoria wouldn't have time to rethink the choices she'd made here, Ben let the men in and helped them carry out boxes. Half an hour later, everything was gone, including the bed, and the day care gift had been picked up. There were only three suitcases left in the tiny apartment.

"I'll take the vacuum down to the car," he offered, eager to get Victoria out of here. The inner happiness he'd admired since the day he'd met her seemed to dim with every moment they remained in this joyless place. It was no wonder she'd made a mistake in love while living here.

"Leave it for the next tenant. All I want are my clothes. Let's go."

"You're the boss." Ben stowed her luggage in the car and returned to find her taking one last look around. "Ready?" At her nod, he slid his hand under her elbow and escorted her down the stairs, Mikey clomping behind them. "Next stop is the hotel."

"This is where we're staying?" she gasped when he drove underground at the West Edmonton Mall. "But Fantasyland Hotel rooms are very expensive."

"They have a deal on," he said nonchalantly. "Besides, staying here means we won't have to go out into the cold again. This mall has everything we need."

"Unca Ben said we can go swimming."

Ben chuckled at Mikey's excitement, glad he'd made the promise. No way would Victoria want to deny the boy time in the famous water park, and no way did he want her to linger on the past. Suitcases in hand, he led the way to the check-in desk, delighted that she didn't argue. It was about time somebody started cosseting Miss Victoria Archer and Ben figured he was the guy to do it.

As it turned out, their decision to visit the water park before dinner was perfect. Victoria's strained expression melted away as she and Mikey giggled and splashed, leaving Ben to rock and roll with the massive waves until he finally returned to his chair exhausted.

"You have a lovely family." A woman reclining on a chaise next to their spot smiled. "Picture perfect."

Dazed by the comment, Ben stared at Victoria who was laughing as she coaxed Mikey to float. He turned to correct the woman. She had left but her words hung there.

A lovely family. Not something he'd ever allowed himself to want. But sitting here, watching two people he cared about, two people he wanted to protect, Ben couldn't remember exactly why having a family was impossible.

Responsibility. Yes, he feared that. Being the one in charge, the one who stood alone to face the consequences. But surely that would be easier if there was another parent, someone against whom you could sound off your ideas, like he often did with Victoria? When he was with her, fears melted away. Things always seemed possible with Victoria present.

As the breaking waves rolled in against his feet, Ben allowed a daydream to grow—someone to share with, laugh with, be sad with. Someone who would cut you some slack if you messed up but would also be there supporting you. Someone who knew you weren't perfect and wouldn't hold your screwups against you. Someone like Victoria.

Ben sat bolt upright on his chair.

"Ben?" Victoria stood in front of him, holding Mikey's hand, her gray eyes confused. "Is something wrong?" Her hair stood in funny little waves and peaks where the water had messed it. She didn't have on a scrap of makeup, her face dripped with water—and she looked utterly beautiful.

"You sick, Unca Ben?" Mikey touched his knee. "You need dinner?"

"Dinner?" Ben licked his lips. "Yeah, that's it." He felt dazed, as if he'd been held under that water too long and now floated in the realm of possibility. *A partner—like Victoria?*

"We came to tell you that we've had enough swimming," she said, her forehead furrowed. "Have you?"

Ben couldn't seem to gather his thoughts, couldn't figure out what Victoria was asking him. Enough? No way! He could never have enough of watching her lovely face or the way she slid a protective arm around Mikey when some rowdy teens almost bumped into him. Ben kept staring, bemused by the warm sensation filling him. Was that love? Or simply affection?

Victoria was fun to be around. She didn't expect anything from him and she accepted him as he was, flaws and all. And yet, something in the way she looked at him urged him to be better, do better, stand taller. That's what he felt for her—admiration. But not only that.

"I'm going to call for medical help if you don't stop staring at me like that, Ben." Victoria grabbed her towel and swathed it around her like a sarong, then did the same for Mikey. Exasperated by his immobility, she reached out a hand and shook his shoulder. "Ben, wake up."

"I'm awake." Feeling foolish but unable to shake off the drug-like feelings that gripped him, he stumbled to his feet and slung his own towel over one shoulder. "I'm ready to go whenever you are, Victoria," he said in a voice that didn't sound like his own. "Did you have fun, Mikey?"

"Yeah. But now I want sa'ghetti." The way Mikey trustingly slid his hand into Ben's finally woke him up.

What if the boy wouldn't accept another family? Somehow it had never dawned on Ben that Mikey might resist his plan. And there in a nutshell was proof that he wasn't parent material. Not like Victoria. She would have thought through all the pros and cons, but top of her list would have been meeting Mikey's needs.

"I'll change and meet you two at the escalator, okay?" Victoria frowned at his slow response. "You're really not sick?"

"I'm fine." Ben led Mikey into a change room. Okay, so he wasn't parent material. But he wasn't stupid, either. All he had to do was follow Victoria's lead and when in doubt, run his concerns past her. Surely if he did that he couldn't fail.

Something was wrong with Ben.

Victoria stewed over it while she showered, dressed and dried her hair. But by the time she met him and Mikey at the escalator, she'd found no answers.

They chose a family-style restaurant and ordered Mikey's favorite spaghetti. It was fresh and tasty, but after a few bites, Victoria pushed away her plate.

"What's wrong?" Ben glanced from her to the plate and back again.

"Exactly what I'm wondering." She kept a bead on him, refusing to look away. "Talk to me, Ben."

He glanced at Mikey and gave a slight shake of his head before mouthing *later*. For now, she would have to be content with that, but she wasn't going to let it go.

"You need some energy after all that work today. You should try to eat a little more," Ben said. She picked up her fork and managed a few more bites. But concern kept gnawing at her, taking away her appetite.

After Victoria finished her bedtime story and Mikey had been tucked into bed and was snoring, she sat down at the desk. She wasn't going to her room until she had an answer.

"What's bothering you, Ben?"

"A whole lot of questions." He sat down opposite her and raked a hand through his hair. "None of which I have the answers to."

"Such as?" Victoria felt cozy and comfortably tired as she stretched her feet out in front of her. Her favorite electric-blue jogging suit was perfect for après swim as she waited to hear Ben's concerns.

"Tillie and Margaret keep telling me to pray

and seek God's way." His shoulders slumped. "I've prayed as hard as I can but I'm still uncertain."

"About?" she asked hopefully.

"Everything. Finding parents." As he glanced at sleeping Mikey his face softened. "Not finding parents."

"*Not* finding parents?" she asked sharply, surprised by the admission.

"I don't want to leave him, Victoria. But I don't think I can care for him. I'm not sure about anything lately," he said plaintively. "All I know is that I love Mikey. I want him to be happy and I'll do whatever it takes to make that happen, *if* I could figure out what that is."

"I don't know if this helps, Ben." Victoria hesitated. But he sounded so tortured by his decision that she had to at least try to help. "But I'm facing some of the same questions."

"You? You're always confident about everything."

"I wish." She frowned. "Like having this baby. Maybe I'm being selfish."

"Selfish?" He shook his head. "You're the most unselfish person I know."

"Nice of you to say, but maybe keeping this baby, raising him myself—maybe that's selfish. Maybe giving him to people who are longing for a child, two parents who can provide everything he needs—" She shook her head. "I have as many questions as you, Ben. The only difference is I refuse to give in to my fears. I intend to keep this child as close to my heart as possible."

"Aren't you afraid you'll mess up?" His blue eyes clouded.

"Of course." She reached out and touched his hand. "But what parent do you know who's perfect? Who doesn't make mistakes? Your brother would probably tell you he and his wife did. But God can turn mistakes into good, like He did by giving me the aunts."

Ben frowned at her, his mind obviously busy. Victoria sat there, waiting for the questions she knew were coming and half-dreading her response because maybe when he knew the truth, he'd think she shouldn't be any kid's mom.

"What mistakes did your parents make?"

"I never knew my father," she said quietly. "I don't think my mother did, either."

"Oh." Ben waited, blue eyes totally focused on her.

Victoria drew her hand from his, inhaled for strength and then said the horrible words.

"My mother was a prostitute."

To his credit, Ben didn't show the revulsion he must be feeling.

"I'm sorry," he said in a gentle voice. "That must have been hard to say."

"I don't think she wanted to be. I don't remember a lot about her, but what I do remember is a woman who craved escape. Alcohol was her method." Ben didn't flinch or turn away as Derek had when she'd told him. Perhaps that emboldened her to continue. "Not that she ever left me hungry or alone. She didn't. I was well cared for."

Victoria couldn't help smiling as small snippets of the past fluttered through her brain. Racing through the park with her mom chasing her in a game of tag. Flying high on the swing set as her mother pushed her. Sitting in her mom's lap, strong arms encircling her and listening to made-up stories about princesses and castles.

Standing alone and afraid in a room with dingy yellow walls, waiting for someone who would love her like her mom.

"How did you end up in the foster system, Victoria?" Ben's voice drew her from that shadowy place.

"She left me there." She smiled at his disbelief. "One morning after breakfast, she dressed me in my very best outfit. Then she told me I was going to be like the fairy princesses and live in a castle. She said she loved me so much, that she always would, but that she had to go away. We walked to a building, she took me inside and left me there."

"But you were just a child!" he gasped. "How old?"

"About the same age as Mikey," she murmured,

smiling at the sleeping child. "Maybe that's why I feel such a connection with him. Maybe by being so determined to keep my own baby, I'm trying to repair something in my past. At least that was Derek's diagnosis."

Ben simply snorted his repugnance for the theory though his expression told her he was troubled by what she'd said. After some silent reflection, he looked directly at her.

"What happened to your mother, Victoria?"

"She died about a week after she left me. Suicide." She appreciated his concerned look. "It's okay, Ben. It happened a long time ago and I was eighteen before I learned the truth."

"How—the aunts," he guessed.

"Yes." Victoria nodded. "I was about to graduate from high school. I was desperate to know more about myself, to figure out my place in the world. A few fragments of memory weren't enough anymore. So Tillie and Margaret hired a private investigator."

"You must have been devastated." His handsome face softened as he watched her.

"Yes, I was. And my history has dogged me for years," Victoria admitted.

"That's why you think you're not good enough to have this baby? Why you often put yourself down, why you push yourself so hard?" he asked in a very quiet voice.

"Maybe." She'd never thought of it in those terms, but she would—later.

"The aunts tried to help. They assured me that The Haven was my castle, the place where I, the princess of God, the King, would always belong. I knew by then that they loved me and that helped me understand and accept their belief that God had led me to them. I've never truly felt I belonged at The Haven though. Still don't. Why me? Why not someone more worthwhile? But I am very grateful to my aunties." She wrapped her arms around her waist as the memory of precious moments with those dear women returned.

"Tell me what you're thinking, Victoria," Ben pleaded softly.

"About when the aunts first brought me to The Haven." She smiled at the warmth that still glowed inside. "I felt so loved, so treasured." She looked at him. "That's what I want my child to feel. I don't ever want him to question whether he belongs."

"He?" Ben asked, a quirky little smile tilting his mouth.

"I call the baby he, but I have no idea whether it's a boy or a girl. That's up to God." She chuckled at herself. "Anyway, the purpose of my trip down memory lane was to say that God took care of me all those years. He led me to the aunts and The Haven so I figure that, until He tells me loud and clear that I may not keep this child, my baby is mine. Somehow I've got to believe He'll work out the rest. That's what I've learned from Auntie Tillie and Margaret."

"Not a bad thing to learn."

"No. But it's not easy, either." Victoria glanced at the clock and rose. "It's getting late. I'm sure you want to rest after such an arduous day. Thank you for everything, Ben. I could never have cleaned the place out myself in an afternoon."

"I'm glad I was finally able to give something back in return for all you've done for Mikey and me." He stood in the doorway, watching as she moved across the hall and slid her key card in the lock of her room. "Sleep well, Victoria. And thank you for sharing your story with me. I'll try to remember to trust God more."

She smiled, nodded and slipped inside. But as she lay in bed, she couldn't wrest her thoughts away from Ben. Until tonight, she hadn't fully appreciated how difficult he was finding the realization that soon he'd have to walk away from his nephew.

"You have a plan, an answer that's good for everyone," she whispered, squeezing her eyes closed as she had at Mikey's age. "Please help Ben find it. Open his heart. Let him stop being afraid to love that little boy."

And me?

Victoria pushed away that silly question. She wasn't a little girl anymore. She knew she wasn't a fairy princess, that no prince charming was going to rush in and rescue her. It wasn't just feelings of unworthiness that reminders of her mother always engendered. In a couple of months, she'd be so huge no man would compliment her. Certainly not Ben. He'd be far away in Africa.

She wanted to feel strong, independent, invulnerable. She worked hard to be just that, to find her own niche in the hotel and excel at her job. To prove she was worthy. Until she'd fallen for Derek, she'd always pretended she was a loner.

But now, lying in this bed, the same old longings she'd felt at eighteen slipped in and grabbed her. She still yearned to be loved in that silly romantic way her mom had described.

"Not gonna happen," Victoria told herself sternly.

She'd become good at pretending it didn't matter that Ben didn't love her. But somewhere inside a little, almost five-year-old Victoria wept for the death of her fairy-tale dream.

"Mikey and I will be fine. We're going to do some shopping. My medical appointment isn't until three," Victoria explained to Ben. "That should give you plenty of time to do what you need to."

Ben almost chuckled. Another reminder, as if he needed it, that this woman was beautiful, strong and, most of all, independent. He couldn't stop staring at her gleaming dark hair, sparkling gray eyes and big wide smile. Gorgeous. And yet, some protective part of him noted tiny fine lines at the corners of her eyes that told him she hadn't slept much. He wondered if she'd overdone it yesterday.

"You'll call if you need me?" he asked, unable to shake a slew of nagging worries.

"Ben, we're going shopping. We won't need help to do that." She chuckled and turned away, her hand sliding into Mikey's. "Bye."

"See ya, Unca Ben," the boy called, churning his little legs to pull her toward a display of toys in a nearby store.

Ben spent several minutes watching them, until he realized folks were watching him. With a shake of his head, he walked to the car then drove to the lawyer's office where he learned the details of settling Neil and Alice's estate were slowly progressing. The insurance office for his rental car was not, however, and it took several hours of insisting he had to retrieve the boxes from the damaged vehicle *today*.

Having finally attained permission, Ben drove to the storage facility and began transferring the white boxes from the trunk of his wreck into the back of Victoria's car. He'd lost track of time when his phone pealed.

"Ben, where are you? It's two thirty. I need to get to the doctor's." Victoria sounded stressed, which he knew from chapter three of the book he'd bought was not good for a mom-to-be.

"I'm sorry, Victoria, but there's no way I can get there in time. How about if you text me the address for your doctor and then take a cab?" he suggested, irritated with himself for messing up. "I'll meet you there. That way you won't be late."

"Okay," she responded. No fuss, just face the issue and solve it. That was Victoria.

"Everything okay? Mikey?" She sounded—what? Anxious? No, more like nervous.

"He's fine. We'll see you there, Ben." There was an unsteadiness there that he didn't like.

"Yes, you will," he said to reassure her. He hung up then hastily finished loading the boxes. Ben slammed the door on the back of her car with a sigh of relief that it had closed. Hopefully Victoria hadn't bought a lot because room inside the vehicle was now at a premium.

Thirty-five minutes later, Ben pulled into a parking space at the rear of the medical clinic, stuffed the meter and then, because the elevator took so long, raced up the stairwell. He was puffing hard by the time he yanked open the fourth-floor door. Victoria was seated by Mikey. Her smile at him was tight.

"Hi."

"Hi, yourself. I'm so sorry, Victoria. I had to drive to the compound where they're storing my rental car to get my things." As he inclined his head toward Mikey, he noticed that her hand was shaking. "What's wrong?"

"My doctor wants to do an ultrasound today," Victoria whispered. Her gray eyes were huge, her oval face pale.

"That's normal, isn't it?" Ben felt totally stupid for asking. Why hadn't he read more in that book he'd bought about pregnancy? How could he support her if he wasn't clued in about what to expect?

"I didn't think it would happen this early." Her hand slid into his and held on as if she needed him. "Ben, would you mind—"

"Victoria Archer." A woman wearing a green polka-dot uniform stood by the check-in desk.

"Will you come with me, Ben?" Victoria asked. "Please?"

"Sure." Surprised that he felt no hesitation about being this involved, Ben rose. Then whispered, "What about Mikey?"

"Victoria?" The woman stood in front of them now. "I'm Eva. Is there a problem?"

"I want Ben with me but Mikey—" Victoria paused.

"Mikey should come along. We have a toy room. He'll love playing there while you see the doctor." Eva grinned at the child then led them to a room at the rear of the office.

With no idea of what was to come, Ben followed. Would they ask him to do something? Help Victoria breathe or something? Whatever she needed, he could do, he told himself.

"Here you go, Mikey. You can play with anything you want, okay? Granny Jo over there will help if you need her. We'll be back there with the doctor."

"Can I fly that plane?" Having received permission, Mikey was quickly engaged in the toy.

Eva directed Victoria to change in a small cubicle then led Ben next door to a dim room with a huge machine. A tiny woman suggested he take a seat, so he obeyed, trying to stifle his nervousness. For Victoria's sake.

Thankfully she soon appeared clad in a white paper gown and her jeans. She climbed onto the table as directed.

"Okay, Miss Victoria. This isn't going to hurt. We'll just put a little of this jelly on your stomach, and then I'll slide this probe around to give us a view of your baby. The doctor wants some good pictures, so we'll snap those, too."

"O-okay." Victoria glanced at him.

Something in her look told Ben to get up, move to the side of the bed and slide his hand over hers.

"Relax," he said softly. "You've had your picture taken before."

"It's not *my* picture they want." She caught her breath as the jelly hit her skin.

"Smile anyway." Ben didn't want to intrude so he kept his gaze on her face while Victoria stared at the monitor.

"There's your baby's heart, Mama," the technician said. "Can you see?"

"Y-yes." Victoria turned to him. "Look, Ben," she whispered through her tears. "It's my baby."

"Uh-huh." He couldn't think of anything to say that would express his wonder at seeing the tiny being on the screen. All he could do was stare and marvel.

"Ben! You're holding too tight." Victoria drew her hand away, stretched her fingers then slid her hand back into his. "Okay?"

"He's just like most daddies," the technician said with a laugh. "Shocked into silence by God's handiwork."

Ben should have corrected her, explained that he was just a friend. But movement of that tiny creature on the screen had indeed silenced him.

He figured Victoria would explain, but her focus was on her baby, her eyes filled with tears.

"Okay, that's great." The technician wiped off the gel. "You can change back into your top and wait for the doctor in the toy room. She shouldn't be long."

"Th-thank you," Victoria sputtered but the lady had already left.

Ben held out his arm for her to use if she needed help to sit up. She took it, rose but didn't look at him.

"I'll, um, get dressed," she whispered.

"I'll stay with Mikey." He touched her hand before she could leave. "Are you all right?"

"Dumbfounded but fine," Victoria murmured with a bemused nod before she scurried out of the room.

That was exactly how Ben felt as he contemplated the enormity of what he'd seen. A baby. Victoria's baby. He couldn't stop grinning.

This must be how Neil had felt on seeing his son. Amazed, daydreaming, imagining future possibilities for Mikey.

But would those dreams ever come true now? Would someone else care enough about his brother's child to ensure it? Ben's grin faded.

Could he really depend on someone else and just walk away? And if things didn't go well, would Mikey understand why he'd left him?

Chapter Ten

Victoria sat silent in the car. She studied the sonogram for a long time before finally tucking the photo into her bag.

"Pretty incredible, huh?" Ben chuckled when she didn't answer. "I've never seen you at a loss for words, Victoria."

"I don't know how to express what I'm feeling." She couldn't stop smiling or touching her stomach.

"Try. In one word," he said as they merged onto the freeway.

"Blessed," she whispered. "So blessed."

"By God. Now hang on to that when those doubts about your worthiness return," Ben ordered with a grin. "One thing you learn in peacekeeping is to savor every good moment because you don't know when the next one will come."

He was just so nice, which made it doubly hard to crush her growing feelings for him.

"When are we gonna be home, Unca Ben?" Mikey asked.

So he considered The Haven home. Victoria's happiness grew. Until a new thought dawned.

"I'm so sorry, Ben. I wasn't thinking. Did you need more time in the city?" She studied his handsome face, still amazed by his reaction when the baby, her baby, appeared on that screen. He hadn't looked disgusted or repulsed. He'd looked like she felt. Stunned. Victoria shook herself back to reality. "We could stay longer if you need to."

"Thank you, but I've got what I need," he said in a firm voice.

"I'm guessing that's why we had to squish our shopping bags around Mikey," she teased.

"I wanted to bring everything." Ben's lips tightened. "Since they promised weeks ago that they'd ship them to me and haven't, and since we were here, I grabbed the opportunity. I'm sorry I didn't get back in time to drive you to the doctor's office, and also that I've taken so much room in the car, but I was afraid to leave anything behind."

"No problem. I guess I never realized they were so important." It was becoming steadily more difficult to stop daydreaming about Ben. He was like a magnet, drawing her attention even when she wasn't with him.

"I'm not sure if all of them are important because I haven't yet gone through everything. I just wanted stuff out of the house so I packed as quickly as I could. I stored most of their things, but there are picture albums and a lot of notebooks in the boxes," he explained. "Neil began journaling when he was in rehab. I hope to go through every one of his journals before I go back to work." His gaze slewed from the road to her and back. "What's in the bags? I didn't think you had enough time to buy so much."

"Vic buyed me new shoes, Unca Ben." Mikey's eyes sparkled. "They gots lights that flash when you walk."

"Wow. You're blessed, too, kiddo." Ben looked at her apologetically. "I've been meaning to get him new shoes—"

"I know, Ben," she said gently. "There isn't much selection in kids' shoes at Chokecherry Hollow. Besides, you needed some personal time. But since we were there and there was a shoe store—" Victoria shrugged. "I seized the moment."

"You've done that a lot for us. Thank you." That generous smile of his did funny things to her pulse. Funny but nice.

Ben certainly was a man to admire, but Victoria was pretty sure her feelings for him were growing way past admiration. She mulled that over while Mikey listened to music on her phone with her earbuds. He soon fell asleep.

The silence that reigned between her and Ben was comfortable. They didn't need to keep a conversation going, just a comment here and there, a nod, a chuckle said it all. Ben understood her. As they finally entered the road toward The Haven, Victoria came to just one conclusion.

Aside from her foster sisters, Ben was the best friend she'd ever had.

"Coming back to The Haven like this—it gives me a warm, comfortable feeling inside," Ben murmured. "I haven't had that feeling for a long time, if ever."

That made her sad, but then Mikey wakened.

"We're home!" he squealed as they stopped in front of the house.

Ben opened his mouth as if to remind his nephew that this wasn't his home, but stopped. He glanced at her and shrugged, a funny little smile lifting his lips as he climbed out. The kid spoke truth.

"Why don't you two go inside?" he said. "I'll unload the car."

"I'll help." Victoria grinned as Mikey raced toward the aunts who were waiting, arms extended. She reached for her suitcase. To her surprise, Ben refused to hand it over.

"You shouldn't be lifting heavy things," he said before striding toward the house, arms brimming.

"Oh, brother." She rolled her eyes then grabbed as many shopping bags as she could carry, walked to the front door and paused in the doorway. "I'm pregnant, Ben, not an invalid," she muttered when they were in the foyer.

"I know." He ignored her huff of disgust, set down the luggage and helped her off with her coat. After a quick grin at her chagrin, he left to retrieve his boxes.

Victoria wasn't going to tell him, but she enjoyed the way he cared for her. So it seemed pointless to argue with him, especially when she couldn't put any heart into it. She turned instead to hug Tillie and Margaret.

"What have you two been up to?" Judging by their excited looks, Victoria wondered if she should be afraid. "What?" she demanded when neither one spoke.

"We have good news for Ben," Tillie said as she clasped her hands together.

"Very good news," Margaret added, and shared a grin with her sister.

"Oka-a-y." Suddenly concerned, Victoria forced herself to remain calm as the aunts suggested Mikey might like to enjoy the milk and fresh chocolate-chip cookies Mrs. Marsh was baking.

Mikey raced toward the kitchen just as Ben returned with the last box.

"That's it. The car's empty," he said as he unzipped his jacket. He paused, arms still inside his sleeves and stared. "What's wrong?"

"Nothing. Everything is perfect." Tillie slid her arm through his. "Dear Ben, we think that we've found the perfect family for Mikey, a couple who are everything you've asked for."

"Plus some things you didn't." Margaret pulled an envelope from her pocket and held it out. "If you'll look this over, I think you'll find we've managed to fulfill every one of your requests."

"Isn't it wonderful, dear?" Tillie asked grabbing her hand.

"Wonderful," Victoria agreed quietly. *Mikey and Ben would be leaving soon.* Her heart sank as Ben perused the document.

"This couple does look good—wait a minute. They're moving to Africa?" Concern darkened his eyes as he studied the two sisters.

"Not right away. They're going as missionaries in September," Margaret explained.

"Which means there will be plenty of time for Mikey to get to know and love them," Tillie said.

"On top of everything, they'll be located only a day's drive from where you're stationed in Africa. Isn't it wonderful?" Tillie's joy filled her face. "God certainly answered our prayers."

Victoria didn't believe Ben thought that. In fact, the longer he studied the papers he'd been given, the less thrilled he looked. Actually, he looked decidedly uncomfortable.

"You'll need time to consider everything." Margaret nodded. "But when you're ready, we'll introduce you. You'll see that Jared and Willa are the perfect parents for your nephew."

"Now let's go have cookies with Mikey. I've missed that child something fierce." Tillie blinked quickly then hurried her sister toward the kitchen.

Ben's silence worried Victoria. She shifted from one foot to the other, waiting for him to say something. Finally anxiety took over. "What's wrong?"

"They seem like good people on paper," he said carefully, lifting the letter. "Energetic, committed, Christians. And they'll offer a lot of the things I asked for. But—" He paused.

"But?" Victoria saw the inner struggle reflected in his darkening gaze.

"I don't want Mikey to go to Africa." Ben folded the paper and slid it into his pocket.

"Why not? It could be great. Think of the wildlife he'll see and the exposure he'll get to—why not?" she repeated curiously.

"Mikey's four. He'll start school next year. Sure, he'll attend the mission school for the first year or two, but then he'll have to go to boarding school, like the other missionary kids stationed in that area."

"How do you know that?" she wondered.

"My friend and I used to volunteer at that mission. We visited often so we got to know a lot of personal details. Especially about their kids. Most of those kids struggled to reconnect with their parents after being away for such long periods." Ben's mouth worked for a moment.

"Oh." That didn't sound ideal.

"Mikey will barely settle into their home and then he'll have another big transition to make when he leaves for school. He'll be separated from his brand-new family and everything will be unfamiliar. That's the opposite of what I want."

"Yes, I see what you mean." Victoria noted the sadness that gripped him and placed a commiserating hand on his arm. "So they're not right. But you can't get discouraged, Ben. I've prayed and prayed about this. God has a solution. We just have to figure out what it is."

But he seemed quieter than usual for the rest of the afternoon and the evening meal. He didn't eat much dinner and he didn't smile or grin during her preposterous and silly bedtime story to Mikey. When the boy was finally sleeping, Ben told Tillie and Margaret his thoughts. Victoria felt sorry for her aunts' dismay as they explained that the couple couldn't have children.

"I'm sure they'd be wonderful parents." Ben's forced smile said he was trying to soften his words. "I know you're trying to help, and I appreciate it more than I can say, but I don't believe this couple is the right solution for Mikey," he said quietly. "I'm sorry."

Victoria waited until he'd excused himself before commiserating with the aunts. Seeing their disappointment, she sought to cheer them up by showing the ultrasound pictures. And it worked. Tillie and Margaret seemed as thrilled as she was and insisted on praying for her and the baby right there. Their steadfast love and concern warmed her heart. As Victoria reveled in their generous affection, she recalled Ben's suggestion that she let go of her feelings of unworthiness and enjoy each day.

He always helped her through the difficult parts. Okay, he wouldn't be leaving right away, but what in the world would she do when Ben was gone?

And more importantly, was there a family out there that Ben would ever approve of? That spurred hope that maybe he wouldn't send Mikey away. Maybe he'd stay, open his shop, build a new life.

Tomorrow she was going to ask him his plans in the event that her aunts didn't find a family for Mikey before he had to leave.

* * *

Even after two months at The Haven, Ben still marveled at Victoria's efficiency. Thanks to her, the volunteer dinner had gone off without a hitch. In fact, folks at the seniors' center in Chokecherry Hollow still talked to him about the funny games she'd led and the amusing prizes they'd won.

Midterm break was another of Victoria's outreaches, which revealed her ease at delving into kids' hearts. She'd invited the local youth group to hold a party at The Haven and skillfully involved them in several activities she intended to use when future foster kids visited. She'd placed saucers of freshly fallen snow with warm maple syrup drizzled over top on the patio picnic table, and then garnished them with chocolate for the culmination of an outdoor evening filled with laughter and camaraderie.

Today she was seated at the kitchen table with Mikey, planning his fifth birthday party and Ben had been called in to assist.

"What do you think about a snowshoe party?" she asked.

"Uh—" Ben hesitated, not wanting to dampen the eagerness that radiated across her face.

"What's that?" Mikey frowned.

"We could make snowshoes and then take a walk with them through the woods," she explained.

"I dunno how to do that." Mikey looked dubious, and Ben didn't blame him. A bunch of five-year-olds learning to make snowshoes seemed a little—too ambitious?

"Okay. Not snowshoeing," Victoria agreed with a sigh. "But you have to give me some idea of what you want, Mikey."

"I want a fire," he said firmly.

"I know. You said that four times. I've got a wiener roast written down. What else?" she nudged.

"I want Unca Ben to make a snow house that me and Garnet c'n play in." Mikey's brown gaze rested on him. "Unca Ben c'n do it. He builds lots of stuff in the army."

"He's a good builder, that's for sure." Victoria's grin sent Ben's insides churning. How he loved that smile. "He and Jake sure built some nice tables for outside."

"I want a snow house. Not wood," Mikey clarified.

"Sounds like an igloo," Ben mumbled and immediately wished he hadn't.

"Yeah!" Mikey jumped up from his chair. "I want a' igloo for my birthday. C'n I have that? Me 'n Garnet could have lots of fun in a' igloo."

"*An* igloo," Victoria corrected automatically. "How about it Ben. Doable?"

"In five days?" Ben swallowed a groan.

He'd applied for an extension to his leave but

had received no response, which meant he was due to leave The Haven in three weeks. His to-do list before leaving included repairing four wonky computers and teaching a class in online security at the seniors' center. Plus he was already working with Jake on making trails in the woods that were supposed to turn into circular hikes for summer guests to enjoy. And he still hadn't gone through all of Neil's journals, let alone found Mikey a home.

But when he looked up and saw the hopeful expression in Victoria's eyes he couldn't refuse.

"Please c'n you make me a-an igloo, Unca Ben?" Mikey wheedled.

"I guess I can try." Ben held up a hand to silence Mikey's whoop of joy. "But it will depend on the weather. If these warm temperatures continue, the snow won't hold together and the igloo won't stay up. You have to be prepared in case that happens."

"I'm gonna ask the aunties to help me pray to God to make it real cold," Mikey declared. "An' we c'n make paper airplanes for decorations." He raced from the room.

"I'm sorry. I probably shouldn't have asked you to make an igloo in front of him," Victoria murmured. "You've got a lot on your plate already."

"Well, it is his fifth birthday and I do want to

do something special for that," he said. "I just wish I knew what to give him for a gift."

"You'll come up with something, but whatever you give him, he'll love it."

"I hope so." Ben suddenly thought of the lovely robe he'd stashed in the back of his closet, the gift he hadn't yet given Victoria. She'd claimed to love the wooden box he'd made her for Valentine's, but somehow the robe now seemed too personal. Perhaps it would be best left as a thank-you-and-goodbye gift.

"Still no answer on your request for a leave extension?" she asked as she gathered her notes.

"No." A sinking feeling took over. "I guess that means they'll say no."

"Olivia works for a Colonel in the military. She files those kinds of requests all the time and she told me they usually try to say yes, especially when it's for compassionate reasons. And—" Victoria winked at him "—the aunts and I have been praying hard so don't give up just yet."

"Okay." He poured himself a cup of coffee and studied the white board lying on the table. "How's the plan going? Wasn't there an inspector here yesterday?"

"Health inspector, yes, and he gave the all clear in regard to this kitchen but..." She peered at the board and frowned.

"But?" he prodded. "What else is bothering

you?" He sat down across from her, glad to see more color in her cheeks. "Let's talk it out, Victoria."

"You're very good at that, aren't you, Ben? It's one thing I really appreciate about you."

"One thing. Huh. Well, I suppose that's better than nothing." That got a smile out of her, which was the goal of his comment. "I like you, too," he added then wondered if he should have said it when her eyes flared wide in surprise.

"Oh. Thank you." She dipped her head and stared at the table, but she couldn't do it for long and soon was peeking through those lush dark lashes. "Want to go for a walk?"

He really didn't. But he could never say no to Victoria, not knowing how much she loved the outdoors.

"Anywhere in particular?" he asked as he dumped his coffee in the sink.

"Yes." Victoria rose and smoothed a hand over her midriff. "But I'd rather show you than tell you."

"Okay." He followed her to the door, held her coat and then donned his own.

"It's a good day for a walk since it's so warm." She giggled when he made a face. "You don't have to work, I promise. I only want your opinion."

"Which will probably lead to work," he said

in his drollest tone. Then lest she misunderstand, he quickly added, "Not that I mind a little work. Mikey and I have stayed here far longer than any guest should."

"Ben!" Victoria paused on the doorstep, her hand on his arm to keep him from moving away. "You're not guests. You're our family," she said in the most natural way as her hand slid into his. "Come on. This way."

Family. His heart thudding at those simple yet profound words, Ben walked beside her without speaking. The hand-holding had become commonplace between them, especially on her walks. He needed to make sure she had support if she stumbled or slipped, though it didn't look like that would happen today with the sun beating down on the rocks and melting the snow.

"Stop here," Victoria ordered after about ten minutes. "Now look."

Ben looked. The view from this vantage point was gorgeous; an almost circular meadow with a stream to one side seemed to be waiting for someone to enjoy it.

"The Haven has a gorgeous setting. I can never get enough of these mountains. Some days, the peaks are covered by silvery clouds that seem to brood with secrets waiting to be discovered, and sometimes they blaze in the sunlight like proud testaments to God's power." He glanced at her, feeling very self-conscious.

"That's beautifully said." Victoria's gray eyes sparkled in the sun's rays as she smiled at him and hugged against his side. "That's exactly how I feel about this place. It's inspiring and daunting at the same time."

Ben slid his arm around her shoulders and felt her head rest against his chest as they stood together, comrades admiring God's handiwork. He smelled the soft lemon scent of her shampoo, felt the satin brush of her dark hair against his cheek, saw her eyes widen as she studied him.

"What are you thinking?" she whispered.

"That I need to tuck this memory away so I can take it out and savor it when I'm back in Africa," he told her very quietly. As if he could ever forget this woman.

"I wish you were staying, Ben." Victoria turned to face him. "You have so much to offer, and I think you'd be a wonderful partner in this work."

"I wish I could." He lifted one hand and brushed the strands of hair out of her eyes. "I wish I never had to leave."

"Then don't." Her gaze held him with an intensity that shook him to his core.

"I have to, Victoria. I have to work."

"There's work here. Lots of it." Her chin jutted out. "You said you wished you could be here to see the kids arrive and leave, to watch their transformation. Then stay. Tell the military you can't come back, that Mikey needs you."

"Mikey doesn't need *me*. He needs a father." Ben eased away from her. "We've talked about it many times, Victoria. You know I can't be the parent he needs."

"I know what you've said." She shoved her hands into her pocket but continued to study him. "Thing is, you can't turn your back on your own nephew just because of something that happened to your brother long ago. You're older, smarter. You'd make different, better choices now, Ben. You'd make a wonderful father."

"You wouldn't think so if—" He bit his lip, hating that he'd kept this secret so long, certain that if Victoria knew the entire terrible truth, he would be her last choice for fatherhood.

"If what?" Exasperation made her eyes glitter and lent a sharp edge to her words. "Let's hear what keeps you from becoming that sweet little boy's father."

"The memory of his father trying to commit suicide. Because of me." Ben couldn't look at Victoria, couldn't watch disgust fill her lovely face. Instead he wandered to a huge boulder that overlooked the valley and sat on it, peering down at the meadow and desperately wishing he didn't have to confess. But he could no longer keep this secret.

Victoria seemed frozen in place, staring at him for several moments before she strode forward and stopped directly in front of him.

"Tell me all of it," she ordered. "Get it into the light of day so we can deal with it. That's what my aunties taught me."

He had to smile at the way she said it, like a little girl who'd confessed to taking a cookie when told not to. How could Victoria ever understand? She'd had a rough life but she'd never had to play the heavy and then feel as if she'd ruined someone's life.

"I'm not leaving until you tell me, Ben."

He sighed heavily then let the details he'd never spoken to anyone flow out from the depths of his heart.

"He was ruining his life, stealing anything he could to pay for his habit but he wouldn't listen, wouldn't let me help him. I realized later that he was trying to escape, trying to blank out the pain. I didn't know it then." He hated saying this, but Victoria nudged her way onto the rock beside him and gripped his hand which gave him courage to continue. "I had a coin collection. Nothing expensive, but I'd had it since I was a little kid. It was the only thing I really valued."

"Neil stole it," she whispered.

"Yes. I confronted him but he had no remorse, no guilt. He needed it and I didn't. I was so angry.

He'd already taken the only two pieces of jewelry my mom had, along with our toaster, our television, anything he could get a dime for. But my coin collection was the last straw." Ben pursed his lips, loathe to go on.

"I can understand that," she stoutly defended.

"Can you understand me telling that miserable little kid that I was disgusted by him, that I wished I didn't have a brother?" he grated.

"I can understand that," she whispered.

Ben couldn't suppress the tears that had lain hidden for so long so he rose and turned his back. He continued the story though, because it was too late to be silent.

"Can you understand me telling him never to come back unless he could return what he'd taken, Victoria?" Ben turned, saw her stricken look and nodded. "Yeah, I can't, either. I crushed my own brother so badly he went to one of his druggie friend's place and deliberately overdosed. He almost succeeded in dying. That's how great a parental figure I am, Victoria. I did that to Mikey's father."

"My dear, dear Ben. You didn't mean to hurt him. You were trying to help." Victoria rested her damp cheek against his as her arms slipped around his neck. "You were barely an adult trying to take care of everyone. You loved Neil the only way you could. You did the very best you could in desperate circumstances. Stop hating yourself."

Ben held her close, craving the comfort she offered even though he knew he could never be forgiven for the mistakes he'd made.

"You loved Neil, Ben, and I believe he knew that. Why else would he have made you Mikey's guardian?" she whispered.

"Because there wasn't anyone else."

"Of course there was." Victoria leaned back to look at him. "If your brother had hated you as you believe you deserve, he'd have made his son a ward of the court. But he didn't. He put you in charge of Mikey because he loved and trusted you would do the right thing for his precious child. He knew that you would do what Neil and Alice couldn't be here to do."

"I'm not sure—" He was afraid to believe what she was saying, afraid to let go of the guilt.

"I am." She brushed her lips against his cheek. "I'm very sure that you are a wonderful, brave man, Ben. You stand up for what's right. You do the necessary, not the expedient. Neil knew that. I believe he considered the matter very carefully and decided, 'My brother, Ben, did his very best for me. Even when I was hard to deal with, he was there, watching out for me, trying to help. I want that for my kid.'"

Ben had never considered anything but that

he'd been chosen because there was no one else. Now he mentally replayed the details of the will and realized the amount of work Neil and Alice had done to ensure *he* was Mikey's guardian.

He blinked back to awareness as Victoria's hand cupped his cheek, loving the silkiness of her touch, tender against his wind-chapped skin.

"You found him, didn't you?" she asked, her voice so tender. "When Neil overdosed, you went looking for him because you loved your brother and you had to make sure he was all right. Didn't you?"

"Yes." He couldn't look away from Victoria's blazing smile.

"Neil didn't hate you, Ben. He loved you as much as you loved him. Let go of the guilt and accept that he never blamed you, that he understood what you did and why."

Then she leaned forward and pressed her lips against his in a kiss that was at once reassuring and exciting and tender and determined and a host of other descriptions that made up this amazing woman.

Ben kissed her back because he couldn't help himself. He adored Victoria's generous spirit and her determination to make the world right for everyone. He tried to express his feelings, hoping he didn't overwhelm her when he felt totally overwhelmed himself.

When she finally took a step back, her gray eyes were wide with surprise. Then she tucked her head into her neck and murmured, "I shouldn't have done that."

"Why not?" he asked boldly, the words bursting out despite his attempt to remain cool and collected. He tucked his finger under her chin and pressed upward so she had to look at him.

"Because—"

"I've wanted to kiss you for a while now, Victoria. Why wouldn't I?" Ben winked, striving for lightness, for his sake as much as for hers. "You're beautiful, and you're a good kisser."

"Because you've had so much experience?" she said tartly as red dots appeared on each cheek. "Mr. World Traveler."

"You're blushing, Victoria." He hid his smile at her discomfiture, tucked her arm into his and turned her toward home. "While we walk back, you can tell me about your plans for that meadow," he said.

Ben pretended to listen as she talked about horses and riders but his brain was focused on Victoria. And the way his heart thudded like a locomotive whenever she was near. He liked her a lot, but that wasn't love.

Was it?

If you loved someone, did you walk away and leave them behind even though everything in you screamed to stay and share whatever the future brought? That's why he'd stuck with Neil through everything. Wasn't that why his brother had left Mikey in his care?

Was that why he didn't want to leave him or Victoria?

Chapter Eleven

"I feel like I'm on a seesaw," Victoria confessed to Darla after Garnet, Mikey, Ben and Darla's husband, Terry, had trooped outside to inspect the birthday igloo Ben had created. "One minute I'm bawling like a baby, the next I'm giggling like a fool."

"If pregnancy was easy—" Her friend paused and chuckled at Victoria's glowering look. "Okay, I won't say it. Just know that you're perfectly normal."

"Is eating a ton of melon normal, too? Because that's what I constantly crave." Just the thought of it made Victoria lick her lips.

"I've heard you enjoy melon with ice cream. Spumoni ice cream." Darla laughed at her surprise. "Terry met Ben in the convenience store in Chokecherry Hollow one evening last week. The poor man was at his wit's end trying to find spumoni. Ben's so sweet. How many men would do that?"

"Not many, I'm sure. Not for someone who's basically a stranger. At least I'm over that phase." Victoria stirred the hot chocolate then poured it into a carafe, hoping to hide her embarrassment. "Now I prefer bubble gum ice cream."

"With melon? Ew!" Darla made a face. "Sorry, but I'd have that reaction to any way bubble gum ice cream is served. And stranger, my foot. Ben's been here almost three months." She arched her eyebrows. "Terry was very impressed by how nice Ben was about driving into town to find it for you. So am I."

"Ben is a nice guy," Victoria agreed. No need to say exactly how nice she found him. "Wait till you see what he got Mikey for his birthday." She ducked her head as her heart rate took off at the memory of that shameful kiss she'd planted on him.

"You're blushing, Victoria," Darla teased then frowned. "You're crazy about Ben."

"Shh. The aunties are here. And I'm not crazy. I just like him. Okay, a lot," Victoria admitted. "Which is stupid of me."

"What is, dear?" Aunt Tillie appeared in the kitchen and promptly forgot her question as she *oohed* over the baby. "May I?" she asked with outstretched arms.

"Sure." Darla handed over her baby daughter. "She loves to be rocked."

"Then we're off to sit in the rocker for a while."

When Aunt Tillie had left, Darla turned to Victoria. "Why is it stupid to like a man—a lot?"

"Isn't it obvious?" Embarrassed to talk about it, Victoria touched her stomach.

"Because you're pregnant?" Darla frowned. "Why does that preclude liking Ben?"

"*Single* and pregnant," Victoria reminded, shrinking inside as she said it. "Not exactly what we talked about when we were in youth group, was it?"

"We didn't exactly discuss me never finishing nurses' training either, Vic," Darla said in a droll tone. "Or about giving up on my first marriage and running back home to lick my wounds. But I did it and I can't undo it."

"That's different."

"How?" Darla shook her head. "Life happened. We both made choices, though not always good ones."

"That's for sure," Victoria mumbled.

"But we can't keep beating ourselves up. Everyone makes mistakes, Vic. It's part of being human, of learning and growing. I don't know about you but I'm not perfect." Darla grinned. "So we ask God for forgiveness and get on with trying to do better."

"That easy?"

"Oh, it's not easy, pal," Darla said grimly. "It's really hard to admit I was so stupid I married a man I knew was an alcoholic because I convinced myself I could help him recover. It's even harder to admit that somewhere down deep inside I knew before I married him that I couldn't. Truth is very painful but you have to face it when your world is falling apart."

"But you loved Randy ever since he and his family moved here when we were in seventh grade," Victoria mused.

"Yes, I did. I told myself love would be enough to show him the way to God. Instead I got dragged down by his unbelief," she sighed, her smile sad. "I knew for a long time that it wasn't going to work, but it took some major events before I could admit that I'd made a mistake, that I'd failed to live up to my dreams."

"That's exactly what happened with me, regarding Derek." Victoria hated remembering how gullible she'd been. "I spent five years believing I loved that man only to realize the Derek I dreamed about was not the man I was in a relationship with. I always knew he had career goals but I thought that he'd change, that I could change him. That a baby would change him."

"Okay, so we made mistakes. But God forgives us and loves us. He knows we're human and He for sure knows we make mistakes." Darla brushed a tear from the corner of her eye. "But thankfully that's not the end of our story. He not only forgave me, He gave me a rich full life that I could never have imagined when I deliberately chose my way over His."

"Yes, but—"

"The Bible says that if we ask, God forgives us, Vic. Period. Who are we to question God's word or beat ourselves up with guilt?" Darla glared at her. "How does guilt help us? Doesn't it make more sense to accept His forgiveness and start again, trusting Him this time instead of ourselves?"

"I guess." The aunts had said the same thing, Victoria remembered. They'd also said God knew before she was born that she'd mess up. They'd suggested she reread Psalm 139. Maybe it was time to do that. After the party. "Do you want to go check out the igloo?"

"Yes!" Darla grinned. "That's why I wore my warmest coat today. Just let me find Tillie."

"Right here, dear." The elderly woman stood in the doorway, the sleeping baby cradled in her arms. "I came to get my afghan. You two girls go have some fun. I'd like to hear this old house ring with your laughter again. This little one and I are returning to the rocking chair by the fire, where it's warm."

Knowing Aunt Margaret was nearby to help, Victoria and Darla donned warm clothes, picked up the carafe of hot chocolate and stepped outside where they paused to admire the igloo Ben had built.

"Wow! Your guy went all out. What a creation and just look at that backdrop." Darla gazed at the vista spread out before them.

"He's *not* my guy," Victoria insisted just above a whisper. "Ben's just a friend."

"Yes, I know that's what you said." Darla's chuckle faded to a frown. "I just want to say one more thing, Vic, honey. For as long as I've known you, you've been proving yourself. I think that's what's holding you back from admitting you love Ben and allowing your love to grow."

"Not sure it's love—"

"It is." Darla ignored her glowering look. "Next time you start thinking you're not worthy, consider this. Does Ben make mistakes? Do you think less of him because he made them? Do you think less of me because of mine?"

"Of course not," Victoria said, a little shocked by the question.

"Then why do you imagine we will think less of you for yours?"

Stunned into silence by the question, Victoria finished their walk, contemplating the thoughts

Darla's question had provoked. But the comment about love would have to wait until she was alone.

When they arrived at the igloo, she ducked her head into the entrance and called, "Permission to enter your igloo, birthday boy?"

Mikey and Garnet gallantly ushered them into the structure and showed off the campfire that vented out the igloo's snow chimney.

"All the modern conveniences, huh?" Funny how she always ended up near Ben, Victoria mused as she sat down on the folded blanket he placed for her and Darla then accepted a steaming cup of the cocoa she'd brought. Her heart did a little dance of happiness. Being near Ben would never get old. "This place is pretty sweet, Mikey. Happy birthday."

"Thanks." The boy gazed at Ben with pure adoration. "Unca Ben's really good at makin' igloos, right?"

"The best," she agreed. Then she couldn't say anything because Ben was gazing at her in a way that made her feel special and cared for and, best of all, pretty. She couldn't look away, either. Didn't want to.

But then Darla cleared her throat and that current between her and Ben seemed to snap.

"So what's the plan, Mikey?" Darla asked in her usual laughing voice. "Are we going to roast some wieners?"

"Yep. Me an' Unca Ben made special sticks for us to use. An' we got marshmallows for s'mores, too." His little face shone with excitement and joy as he glanced at Ben. "I love campfires."

"And wiener roasts and s'mores and Garnet and..." Victoria tickled the boy until he squealed for mercy. This time, she made sure she didn't gawk at Ben. And as far as she could tell, he didn't gawk at her, either. Well, why would he? He'd said she was a good kisser, but he was probably just being nice.

Somewhat chastened by that thought, Victoria munched on her hot dog and let the others do the talking until the campfire had burned down to a few glowing coals.

"When are you gonna open your gifts?" Garnet whispered in a loud voice. "I got you—"

"Garnet," his mother admonished.

"Oops! I almost told you." The boy grinned at Mikey. "Hey, how come you didn't invite some kids from our Sunday school class?"

"'Cause I 'vited you," Mikey said. "An' Unca Ben an' Vic an' Aunt Tillie an' Aunt Margaret. I got lotsa people at my birthday, Garnet. No more would fit in my igloo."

That made everyone laugh. After the wiener roast and s'mores, they all trouped back to the house where Mikey carefully opened each gift and heaped lavish praise on the giver.

"Boots?" he said when he'd torn the paper off a box Victoria had given him. "Unca Ben said winter's just about over."

"These are hiking boots, honey. Now you and I can go tromping through the woods in any season and not get our feet wet, no matter if it's winter or summer," she explained, hoping Ben would notice her reference to the future. "And that orange vest is for you to wear so we can see you through the trees more easily."

"'Cause you know'd I really like walking in the woods, right, Vic?" Mikey thanked her with a tight hug and a kiss against her cheek. "An' I like the game you gived me at breakfast this morning, too," he whispered in her ear.

"You're welcome, sweetie." She leaned back in her chair to watch as Mikey, having saved *Unca* Ben's gift till last, used careful fingers to slip off the ribbon and the paper.

"It's a box," he said as he lifted it up.

"Don't shake it," Ben said quickly. He grinned at Mikey's surprise. "You'll see why when you open it. Go ahead."

"It's a helachopper." Mikey gaped at the small remote control.

"Helicopter," Ben quietly corrected. Victoria held her breath as an inexplicable expression filled the boy's face. "It flies when you push the buttons on this little box. Do you like it?" The big man looked worried by Mikey's silence.

"I like it but I don't think I c'n have it, Unca Ben. My mom—" Suddenly the boy began to sob as if his heart would break.

"What's wrong, Mikey?" Gathering the child into his arms, Ben sat down with Mikey on his knee. "You can tell me."

Victoria squeezed her fingers around the wooden arm of her chair, forcing herself to remain where she was, though she wanted to race to Mikey and embrace him as tightly as she could. But something inside of her said this moment could offer Ben a chance to prove to himself and Mikey that he could handle parenting.

"What's this about your mom, Mikey?" he murmured, his voice oozing tenderness.

"When I asked my mommy for a helachopper before, she said I was too little. Now I'm bigger but my mommy can't never give me one 'cause she's gone to live in God's house," Mikey sobbed. "I don't want God to have my mommy and daddy," he wailed.

"I want your mom and dad here, too," Ben soothed as he brushed his hand against the boy's back, his voice brimming with sadness.

"You do?" Mikey blinked and straightened up to stare at him.

"Sure. I loved your mom a lot, Mikey," Ben

brushed the flop of hair off the child's forehead and pressed a kiss there. "She was very special. So was your daddy." Ben didn't seem to notice the audience listening. His total focus was on the boy.

"Did you have a nice mommy, Unca Ben?" Mikey's concern was obvious.

"Oh, yes, but she went away a long time ago," Ben said.

"An' now you get lonesome like me 'cause you don't gots a mom no more." Mikey nodded understandingly. "That hurts."

"It sure does. But when I came to visit, your mom always made me feel better. She had the best laugh. Do you remember it, Mikey? She'd start giggling and then before you knew it, she'd have tears rolling down her cheeks because she was laughing so hard."

"Yeah, an' she'd bend over and hold her tummy like this." Mikey demonstrated.

"Exactly." Ben smiled, obviously deep into his memories. "And then your dad would start making goofy faces and pretty soon we'd all be laughing."

Victoria watched in fascination as the big soldier gently elicited a host of reminiscences for Mikey that made him chuckle fondly as he recalled his family and their happy times together. She listened avidly to the conversation, feeling like bawling, but refusing to shed a single tear.

Instead she swelled with pride as Ben used gentle humor to ease Mikey out of his sadness.

"Your parents were goofy, Mikey," he teased now.

"I know. 'Member how Daddy used to lie on the floor on his tummy so he could get his crok'ole thing to shoot straight?" Mikey laughed out loud.

"And it never worked, did it?" Was she the only one to notice that, for a second, a flicker of sadness darkened Ben's eyes?

"Nope. He'd shoot and it'd go *ping* and fly under the couch and he'd have to go huntin' for it," Mikey laughed.

"Your dad sure loved to play crokinole," Ben murmured.

"An' 'member how Mommy used to burn the toast?" Mikey was really getting into it now. "When she started singing, she forgot all about our toast."

"I don't think I want to remember that toast, Mikey." Ben's very dry tone made the little boy laugh out loud.

"That's when Daddy gived me cereal." Mikey studied him. "God was nice to give me such a good mommy an' daddy, right, Unca Ben?"

"He sure was. Very good. And that's why I wanted to give you the helicopter for your birthday," Ben explained. "Last year, your mom was right. You were too little. But this year you're five. Much older. It says right on the box that five-year-olds can play with this helicopter so I know your mom would say it's okay."

"But I dunno how it works," Mikey said as he climbed off his uncle's knee. His fingers slid into the older man's. "C'n you show me?"

"Sure I can." Ben rose.

"But Unca Ben, what if I crash it like Daddy's crok'ole thing?" Mikey's eyes grew huge.

"You won't. I'll teach you and Garnet how to fly." Ben smiled at Garnet's squeal.

"I didn't know it's Garnet's birthday, too," Mikey said in surprise.

"Well, I don't think it's actually today," Ben explained as he led the pair to the back door with everyone following. "But we can pretend it is. That way you can have fun flying together. It's always more fun to do things with your friends."

"Yeah." Mikey flung his arm around Garnet's shoulders and grinned at him. "Wanna fly my helachopper?"

"Yeah." Garnet's expression said that was a dumb question.

"He won't need to fly yours. Put your clothes on, boys. Terry, you coming?" Ben grinned at Garnet's father before sliding a second helicopter box off a high shelf. "You and Garnet can use this one."

"I don't know how much help I'll be but I'm coming anyway," Terry assured him.

The aunts went to the window with Darla and Victoria close behind. Together they watched two little boys and two grown men play with one bright red and one bright green *helachopper*.

"Ben and Mikey belong together. Mikey needs him to be his daddy." Victoria couldn't keep the words inside. "Why can't Ben see that?"

"They have a special bond, all right." Darla hugged her as Mikey's toy took a nosedive. "You and I need to do some heavy praying and ask God to open that man's eyes so he won't make a bigger mistake than either you or I have."

"We'll all pray," Aunt Margaret said. "Tillie, you lead."

"How can a five-year-old's birthday party be so exhausting when there were only two kids?" Ben stretched his legs toward the fire in the family room and smothered a yawn.

"It was a great party." Victoria studied him in that way that said she had something on her mind. Immediately his guard went up. "Ben, you can't—"

"Don't. Please?" he sighed. "Not now. I can't argue about leaving him now. I'm weak and vulnerable after all that reminiscing."

"I wasn't going to argue," she bristled. "I was

going to compliment you on how you handled his grief. No natural father could have done better."

"Really?" A rush of pleasure surged inside. "Thank you. I felt like I was walking on eggshells the whole time, but I don't want Mikey to forget about Alice and Neil. I want him to cherish those memories."

"But he will forget, Ben," Victoria murmured. Her smoky gaze moved from the fire to meet his. "With no one to talk about his parents, Mikey is going to lose those precious memories."

"I know." He bit his lip, feeling more helpless than he ever had before. He didn't want to leave Mikey without any trace of his own family, didn't want to give up his right to protect Neil's son.

Perhaps his success earlier with soothing Mikey was what made the crazy idea flickering in the depths of his subconscious seem plausible, even possible. Maybe he could be a real parent. Maybe Chokecherry Hollow could support a store like the one he wanted to open. It would certainly be a great town for a little boy to grow up in.

And Victoria would be nearby. That was the biggest plus.

He'd have to pray about it first, and then talk to Tillie and Margaret. Deep inside, he didn't truly believe there was a way for him to be Mikey's dad but—

"There's a letter for you, Ben." Tillie held out an envelope with an official marking on it.

"Thanks." He tore it open, studied the contents and then grinned. "My leave has been extended until the first week of August." Relief filled him. He could stay, check out possibilities for the future, do more calculations to see if the dream was achievable.

And he could be here to help Victoria with the aunts' retreat dream.

"I'm so glad you'll stay till then." Victoria stood in front of him, her smile as wide as he'd ever seen it. Did that mean she was feeling even a fraction of the attraction he felt for her?

"Not sure." Then he frowned. "Maybe I should find another place. Mikey and I are a burden on you when you're so busy."

"But it's only a few more months," she said, her frown evidencing how much she disliked the idea. "Weren't you the one who protested about getting Mikey settled and then moving him?"

"Yes," he conceded. "But—"

"Do I need to get Aunt Maggie on your case?" The way Victoria's lips twitched told Ben she was joking and yet he felt nervous at the thought. "She can be very persuasive."

"Don't I know it?" Ben grimaced at her reference to a certain senior who'd required several sessions before she could master transferring her pictures to her computer. But for Margaret's persistence, he might have given up.

"Seriously it's much easier to work on their outreach program if you're here than it would be if we had to travel back and forth to confer on things." Victoria winked at him. "Speaking of which—I wonder if you'd look at this and tell me what you think."

He glanced at the sheet she'd retrieved from a drawer and saw a map of The Haven with various areas identified as possible activity areas.

"Where and how did you manage to do this?" He couldn't believe the work she'd put into it.

"Aunt Margaret's new computer came with a program that's perfect for this." As Victoria leaned over one shoulder to point out the changes she'd made since their last conversation, Ben caught the fresh scent of her shampoo—lemon, of course. It was so Victoria—tart with a zing that made you sit up and notice her. "I thought we might put up some type of rope-climbing apparatus for younger kids. We don't know, after all, what age groups we'll have."

"The arrangement of these spaces is very clever," he said, trying to slow his racing pulse, which Victoria's proximity always triggered. "How did you decide it?"

"I found an original topographical map done for the federal government. I scanned it then put it into Aunt Margaret's program." She shrugged her narrow shoulders, covered in a pale gray angora sweater that reflected the exact shade of her eyes. "Once the hills and depressions were outlined, it was easy to figure out what should go where."

"Each is situated in easy reach of the main house and the cabins. It's genius." Ben studied it as thoroughly as he'd have studied a map of any area he was assigned to protect. "I think Jake and I should make some benches for a central rest space here and here," he said pointing. "And maybe some picnic tables by where you indicate a campfire."

"Perfect." Her smile was all the thanks he needed. "So if we have these eight areas selected, the next step would be to order the equipment to use in them. For once the aunts don't have a contact, so I guess we'll have to play it by ear."

"It just so happens I might know someone." A rush of pleasure filled Ben. Maybe for once he'd be able to give back. "My old CO—commanding officer," he clarified when her frown appeared. "He resigned from the service to take over his family's company. Recreational equipment," he elucidated.

Victoria's grin of appreciation was a sight to behold.

"Another answered prayer," she whispered. "I'm so glad you're at The Haven, Ben. I would have had no idea how to move forward. In fact, I've been hesitating, waiting for God to show me. I guess He just did."

"I'll give Marcus a call tomorrow and see what he suggests," Ben promised. "If their company can't do it, he'll know who can."

"That's going to help me sleep tonight," she said and immediately yawned. "Sorry."

"I've been wanting to ask—how are you feeling these days?" Ben didn't want to intrude but he had to know if there was something more he could do for her.

"I think I'm beginning to return to normal," she said with a chuckle. "At least I'm now only occasionally sick. I asked my doctor to transfer my files to Chokecherry Hollow's medical clinic. I'll go in a month or so, but I'm sure everything's fine."

"You look good," he said, mentally altering *good* to *radiant*. Victoria's skin glowed with a luminescence that made her even more lovely than usual.

"Thanks, Ben." Her face flooded with pink. "Though having seen me at my worst, I think anything would be an improvement."

"When are you due, if you don't mind telling me?"

"Why would I mind?" She blinked in surprise.

"September first, though I read first babies are often late in arriving."

"I read that, too." Now Ben was the one whose face turned red. "I wanted to be prepared to help if you needed it so I bought a book," he admitted, wondering if this was the time to give her the robe. No, not yet. "It's fascinating."

Her face showed skepticism and uncertainty before she ducked her head to avoid his gaze.

"Have you thought of names?" he asked, to change the subject.

"Peter if it's a boy." Victoria's eyes softened. "After Peter in the Bible. He was such a great disciple. Impetuous, maybe. But he was utterly devoted to his Lord. I love that he jumped out of the boat to walk with Jesus and didn't even think about the consequences."

"Until he was actually on the water," Ben chuckled.

"At least he did it. Most of us wouldn't get out of the boat," she defended.

"True. And if it's a girl?" Ben couldn't look away. Victoria's whole face underwent a change, seemed to soften, her gaze focused on something not visible to anyone else.

"I'm not sure," she whispered. "I'd like to name her after my mom, but one day she'll learn about her and maybe—" She paused, sighed. "My mom had such a sad life, Ben. I want my little girl to be happy. I don't ever want to cause her shame or embarrassment." Big fat tears fell down her cheeks as she stared at him. "I want my child to be proud of me, but what child would be proud of a mother like me who—"

"Stop it, Victoria." Ben rose, walked over to her and drew her into his arms, softening his voice as he brushed his hand down her back in soothing gestures. "Your child is going to be just as proud of you as you are of him or her. You'll be bursting your buttons as he learns patience and love and generosity and sweetness. You'll be passing on all the things your mom and the aunts taught that's made you the most wonderful, kind, big-hearted woman you are. But mostly everything you teach will be given with God's love and that's all your child will need."

She blubbered on his shirt for a moment, face pressed against his chest. Finally she exhaled, tilted her head back and studied him. "Really, Ben?"

"Absolutely. Are you kidding me? Your child is going to be envied by others," he assured her, knowing that having Victoria as his mom was a blessing no one could take away. "For once and for all, please get rid of this inferiority thing you have about being worthy. You're a beautiful woman who is going to be a fantastic mom. You give love freely and are *worthy* of love."

Something in Ben compelled him to bend his head and kiss her, not a gentle, friendly kiss like they'd shared before, but a real kiss that said he was a man who appreciated her as a woman. A kiss that came from his heart and he hoped showed that he thought her eminently qualified for love.

At first, Victoria seemed startled, but then she kissed him back and Ben loved her response. There was need and tenderness and caring in her kiss, and when at last she eased out of his arms, said good-night and left the room, the only thing he knew for sure was that it hadn't gone on long enough to satisfy the ache in his heart.

He wanted more from Victoria. He wanted her to love him as he now realized he loved her. Which was utterly stupid. If he couldn't be Mikey's Dad, how in the world could he possibly be the kind of man Victoria would need?

And now Ben was here until August, several more months of being near Victoria, sharing her goal of making The Haven a refuge. Days, weeks and months of watching her change, become more confident, more beautiful.

And then he'd have to leave.

Why did You bring me to The Haven, God?

Chapter Twelve

"Not exactly your typical Easter sunrise service." Out of habit, Victoria grabbed Ben's arm for support as they crunched over the crusted bits of snow, not worried in the least that they trailed the end of the line of people who ranged in a line from the mountain's summit to The Haven.

"But great just the same," Ben said. "Very memorable."

"I'm glad they extended your leave." She couldn't help admiring the sharp angle of his jaw and his regal bearing as they walked through the brilliant April sunshine. "I don't think I could have managed a trial weekend for all these kids without your help."

"You're kidding. You, the *no-problem* lady who thinks forty people for dinner is a breeze?" he said, tongue in cheek, eyebrows raised. "You were worried about fifteen giggly preteens? I don't believe it."

"Believe that I was scared stiff they'd beg to go home after the first half hour." She grinned, thrilled by their accomplishment. "But they didn't, thanks to you, Ben."

"No thanks needed," he said with that whole-face-grin that made her pulse gallop. "It's a relief that some of the snow lasted long enough for us to go through with sliding, skating, cross-country skiing and hayrides. But being here with you, watching spring make her melting debut on Easter morning, is amazing."

There was a certain intimacy in his words that reminded her of his kiss after Mikey's birthday and of the hours they'd spent at the kitchen table planning this Easter retreat weekend for foster kids.

"Watching you ride that horse yesterday was more than enough repayment," he added, blue eyes crinkling at the corners. "Your face lit up like a Christmas tree. You might have noticed I couldn't stop staring."

Victoria blushed, heat stinging her cheeks, but she couldn't look away because his gaze held hers. "I did notice," she murmured. "I thought my mascara had run."

"You always look gorgeous to me, Victoria." Ben turned to wave at Mikey who had scooted ahead of them and was now jumping off boulders along the pathway. "Later, after the kids have gone, can I talk to you? Privately?"

"Sure." She was surprised by the request. "Is anything wrong?"

"No. It's just that I've been reading Neil's journals and doing a lot of praying and I want to run something by you."

"Why me?" she asked with a blink of surprise.

"Because I trust that your answer will be honest, not just what I want to hear." His fingers slid to hers and threaded between them. "Because I trust you, Victoria."

"Well, thank you." Funny how much pleasure she found in those words and his touch.

She was curious to hear his thoughts, but at The Haven, with the clamor of the kids over breakfast, there was very little time for any personal talk. After that, they loaded together into a large van and Ben drove them all to church, except the aunts who'd already left because they were performing a special Easter duet. The little white church now felt welcoming, especially as the heady fragrance of potted lilies filled the sanctuary, punctuated here and there by groupings of daffodils and hyacinths. Ben had never felt so perfectly at home.

"Such vivid displays make Easter even more special," Ben whispered as they took their seats.

"I can almost guarantee those are from Aunt Margaret's greenhouse. She has ten green fingers. Probably toes, too." Victoria spent the next few minutes explaining to Mikey that she didn't mean her aunt *actually* had green fingers and toes. She also assured him that he wasn't missing kids' church because there wasn't any today. Then the choir entered and the service began.

As they sang the beautiful, timeless hymns, the congregation seemed to experience the same reverence she did. The music touched Victoria's soul as it delineated the Easter story. Then the aunts rose to perform their duet. Victoria had heard it several times over the years, yet the beauty of their perfectly blended voices brought tears to her eyes as they told the story of Christ rising from the dead.

"Are you okay?" Ben whispered.

Victoria could only nod. As if he understood, Ben slid his arm around her shoulders, comforting her. But comfort was hard to come by as her guilt swelled.

How could she have betrayed her Lord and what she believed? How could she have let herself think she could have a future with a man who didn't believe Jesus had lived or died? Shame swamped her so she couldn't bear to look at the two women who'd given her nothing but love. Despite everything the aunts and Ben had helped her understand, she still felt utterly unworthy.

"The message of Easter is forgiveness. No matter what or where or when or how, your Father forgives you. Because He loves you. Period. That is the meaning of Easter. 'For God so loved the world that He gave His only son.'" The pastor's voice echoed around the sanctuary. "He came so that you don't have to experience the same forty lashes He received, so that you don't have to be hung on a cross, no matter how much you believe you deserve it."

Shocked, Victoria stared at the man behind the pulpit. She'd heard this sermon before. And yet, it was as if the words rang through the building new and fresh, like the spring flowers.

You are forgiven.

"You messed up, dear one. But God isn't mad at you. He doesn't hate you or expect you to endlessly suffer for your mistakes. God feels your pain. His heart hurts that you're suffering for your mistakes." The pastor's voice softened. "But the hurt, the pain isn't His primary concern. What our God is most concerned about, what He desires more than anything, is that you repair your relationship with Him."

A bubble of joy built inside Victoria as those words penetrated her heart and began to thaw the icy barrier that had grown inside.

"The desire of God's heart is that you and He rebuild that sweet communion you used to share. That's what really matters to God," the pastor insisted. "He's not after His pound of flesh. He couldn't care less about retribution. He's after your heart. That's why He gave us His only son. Out of love. What do you want from God this Easter, friend?"

The words hung in the air, challenging yet full of comfort. As they rose to sing a familiar Easter hymn in closing, Victoria felt as if she'd emerged from a cocoon. As if spring's breath had pushed away her chrysalis so that she could breathe and live and feel worthy once more.

The freedom of forgiveness clung to her all through the meal the church put on for the visiting youth. It stayed stuck in her heart as she said goodbye to each precious child and watched them board the bus with smiling faces. It remained through Mikey's chatter as Ben helped with cleanup.

God forgave her. The message sunk its roots deep into her head and played round and round in the sweetest refrain. *Not guilty.* While Ben and Mikey played checkers, Victoria slipped out for a walk, ending up on the summit where they'd held their sunrise service.

"I'm forgiven," she whispered to herself, stunned by the enormity of God's love for her.

"Thank You. I do want our relationship restored but my emotions are all over the place. Maybe that's why I'm so confused about Ben. I'm attracted to him, God. But I don't want to be. I want my focus to be on You, on repairing our relationship. Besides, Ben's leaving."

But even as she said it, she knew that wasn't the biggest problem she faced.

"I don't want to get involved with anyone until I know for sure that's Your will," she said out loud so the words would stick in her mind. "I love being with Ben. I enjoy his touch, his kisses. And You know I love Mikey. But I don't want to make another mistake. So I'll trust You. In all my ways, I'll acknowledge You and You will direct my paths."

Trust. That was the bottom line.

Victoria spent another twenty minutes talking to her Heavenly Father. Then she headed back toward The Haven, relishing the warm kiss of the sun on her face and the longer hours of daylight. She was surprised to find Ben waiting for her at the beginning of the path.

"Am I late for dinner?" she asked with a laugh that quickly died at the seriousness on his face. "What's wrong?"

"Nothing's wrong. I just need to talk to you. Are you frozen or can you walk a bit longer?" he asked quietly.

"Frozen?" she scoffed. "Ben, this is springtime in the Rockies. Perfect weather." She debated whether to pull her hand from his when his fingers closed around it but decided not to. "What's up?"

"I want to talk to you about Mikey." The seriousness of his voice told her he'd come to a decision. Victoria sent up a silent prayer. "I still feel he needs a family, two parents and a home. And I still feel I can't give him that. I want to, more than anything. But I can't."

"Oh, Ben." She wanted to cry for both of them.

"Hear me out, please?"

She sniffed then nodded.

"Everything I've read in Neil's journals so far makes me believe my decision to find Mikey a home is the right one. Neil talks a lot about his family, how much he loved them and wanted Mikey to have the childhood he didn't." He swallowed hard. "The parenting I didn't give."

"I doubt he said that," she butted in.

"Maybe not in those exact words but that's what he meant," Ben sighed. "But I'm also aware that to try and place Mikey in a home in as rushed a fashion as I've been attempting is wrong. That kind of decision needs to be carefully thought through. So what I'm asking you for is time."

"Me?" She stared at him.

"Yes, you, Victoria. You've shown me in so

many ways these past few months that you are a great parent. You love Mikey, which is most important, and you are extremely adept at understanding what he needs." He exhaled before continuing. "I am asking if you will care for Mikey while I return to Africa. Be his guardian, love him as if he's your own until I can come back."

"But—" She frowned. "Ben, you sound as if you're leaving tomorrow. Your leave was extended. You'll be here for months yet." The slow shaking of his dark head tied her stomach in knots. "You won't?"

"I've been recalled, Victoria. I can't give details but there was an uprising and I'm needed. I don't want to go. We've got so much left to plan." He smoothed her hair back from her face. "I've just begun to know you. There's so much I want to share with you, for you to share with me. But—my friends are in trouble and they need me."

"When?" she whispered, afraid to hear it.

"They're sending someone to pick me up tomorrow."

She caught her breath, aghast at the news. Ben couldn't go. He might be injured, even killed. She couldn't lose him.

"I've come to care a great deal for you, Victoria Archer. You're very special to me." He'd let go of her hand so his palms could frame her face.

"I want to stay here at The Haven, to work on the project with you, to share the changing of lives. But apparently that's not what God wants, so I need someone to look after Mikey and you're the one I trust. Will you?"

"Of course. I love him, but Ben, how—" She didn't get a chance to finish because his lips covered hers in a soft but firm kiss.

"Thank you. I appreciate that. You have no idea how much easier it will be to leave knowing Mikey is safe here with you and your aunts. God has provided the very best caregivers he could have in you three."

"Please don't go, Ben." The words tumbled out despite her resolve not to say them.

"I have to. I couldn't live with myself if I didn't help my friends when I've been asked."

"Help how?" she demanded.

"I'm sorry. I can't tell you." Instead he snuggled her against his chest, pressing her head close, murmuring the words he thought would help her understand.

Except Victoria didn't understand.

"I've been in Africa longer than any of them. I know the language, the locals and the customs. I know how to get information." Ben's expression turned grim. "I have to go. But I'll only go knowing Mikey's with you, that you'll love him and care for him."

"Of course I will. But what if—?" She could hardly bear to say it.

"If something happens to me, you will become his permanent guardian. The papers are being drawn up now and we'll sign them before I leave tomorrow morning. Okay?" He drew back, studied her face, blue eyes dark, intense. "Victoria?"

"Yes, but you must come back, Ben. You have to." She wrapped her arms around his waist and held on as tightly as she could, wishing that would make this nightmare go away. "We need you here."

"We have to trust God, Victoria." Ben's solemn tone stopped her cold.

Wasn't that what she'd just told God, that she'd trust Him? So was this a test?

"We have to trust that He has a reason for this, a reason we can't understand. And that He is working it out through us." He brushed his lips against her forehead then continued. "I'll email you when I can. We'll do Facetime and your aunts will write to me every day. We'll keep in touch. You'll tell me all about the project and I'll give you suggestions, which you probably won't take," he teased, bussing her nose.

"I will." She put on a happy face despite the deep misgivings inside. "Then if your ideas don't work out, I'll blame you."

"I know." He didn't smile as he studied her. Instead his face was utterly serious. "I care about you, Victoria. I don't know where that's leading, but I want you to know that you're the person I trust most. Maybe when I come back, we can talk more."

"I'd like that," she said, hoping they'd do more than talk. Then, "Do the aunts know? Mikey?"

"No. I only just got off the phone with headquarters and came to find you." He cupped her face again, his blue eyes holding hers, peering into their depths. "I don't want sadness, Victoria. I don't want crying or Mikey upset. I don't want him to get nightmares thinking I won't be back." His hands slid down her arms and grasped hers tightly. *"Because I will return."*

"I know," she said quietly. Turning, she walked with him toward The Haven.

But she didn't *know.* Her world had been totally upset and now the one man she'd come to trust, her rock, was leaving.

Ben ushered her inside, helped with her coat and then led her toward the kitchen where they could hear Tillie and Margaret talking to Mikey.

"Trust, Victoria," Ben whispered, his breath moving her hair and grazing her skin. "Trust God and me."

Hand in hand, they entered the room to tell the others the news.

* * *

The next morning, Ben took a deep breath before he walked to the kitchen. With sleep elusive, he'd spent hours in prayer, using every breath to beg God to keep Mikey and Victoria safe, to care for them when he could not, to bring him back. But he still didn't feel the assurance he wanted before leaving.

Breakfast was a difficult meal for Ben. Victoria tried to pretend normalcy while Mikey was subdued. Only the aunties seemed relaxed. Part of him wanted to leave quick and fast, as he always had before. Get the goodbyes over with. But a different part, a new Ben, wanted to savor every last second with Mikey and the aunts, but especially with Victoria. He wanted to glue the memories into his brain so he could take them out later and remember every detail. As if they were his family.

"I don't know when I'll have such a delicious meal again," he said after thanking Tillie and Margaret for the waffles with fresh strawberries.

"C'n you send me letters, Unca Ben?" Mikey asked solemnly. "Ones with *pitchers* like you sended Daddy."

"Postcards. Sure, but it takes a long time to get from Africa to here," he explained. "You have to be patient, Mikey."

"'Kay."

"Keep in touch with us, also," Margaret said. "We'll use my computer just like you showed me. I'm very glad I got it."

"So am I," Ben told her with a chuckle, knowing she especially liked the games. As he sipped his coffee with the morning sun streaming over Victoria, time seemed to lag. And then, suddenly, a knock came and there was no time left.

The papers granting Victoria full custody of Mikey in Ben's absence were presented. Ben signed them then waited for Victoria. As his eyes met hers he saw fear and hesitation.

"You're going to do just fine," he said softly so only she could hear.

"I'll do my best, Ben." Her gaze met his, clear, focused. Then she scrawled her signature.

"Thank you." He asked the driver who would take him to the airport to sign as a witness. That finished, he folded the sheets and tucked them into Victoria's hand for safekeeping. "I guess you get to practice motherhood early," he joked. Face solemn, she nodded. Ben turned to Jake and shook his hand.

"Thanks for all your help, man." Jake slapped him on the shoulder. "Be safe."

"I'll try." Ben then wrapped Mikey in a bear hug. "You take care of these ladies, son. I'm counting on you."

"I c'n do it, Unca Ben. I'm five now, 'member?" Chest puffed out, the little boy hugged him back, his embrace so sweet Ben had to blink away tears. How it hurt to leave this child.

"I love you, Mikey," he whispered as he set his nephew down.

"Love you, too, Unca Ben." Mikey's hand reached to grab his as he asked anxiously, "You're comin' back here, right, Unca Ben?"

"You betcha." Ben ruffled the boy's hair, praying he'd be able to keep this promise. "You help Victoria and practice with Garnet on your helicopter. You'll be an expert when I return." He couldn't think how else to reassure the boy so he moved on to the aunties. "Thank you so much for your hospitality and for letting Mikey stay. You have no idea how much it's meant to us to be here."

Tillie smiled, glanced at Victoria and then nodded at her sister who said, "I think we have some idea, Ben. Come back soon. You're part of The Haven now, part of our family." They both embraced him, prayed a quick prayer and wished him Godspeed.

Victoria stood at the end of the line, this precious woman who'd slipped her way into his world and become so much a part of it.

"I don't know what to say to you, Victoria," he admitted softly. "Except, remember that according to God you're worth loving." But he couldn't stop there. "Know that I admire and care about you and want only the best for you. Take care of yourself and your little one."

He stopped because he'd skated as far as he could around what his heart was screaming to say. But he could not, would not say it. He couldn't take the risk of that responsibility. Victoria silently studied him, her gaze holding his until his driver cleared his throat.

"You've been a true blessing, Ben," she finally said in a strong, sincere tone. "Go with God and then come back to us. We love you." Then she stood on her tiptoes and kissed him so sweetly his knees almost buckled.

Ben's heart galloped as his arms swept around her. He kissed her back, pouring everything he couldn't say into that kiss, holding her and wishing he didn't have to let go. Her response almost made him believe he could take on the responsibility that love brought.

But then Victoria drew away, smiled and said, "Don't worry about Mikey, Ben. He's part of our family, just like you."

Part of our family. The repeated words resonated inside him.

To be part of a family, risk the responsibility that came with that—was that what he really wanted? The quick denial that had risen so swiftly when he first arrived at The Haven just wasn't there anymore. He loved this place, cared deeply for the people who lived here but—

"Sir? The commander said you cannot miss that plane." The driver glanced at his watch meaningfully.

"Right." Probably best not to say anything about his feelings when he didn't know what the future held, when or even if he'd return. Ben let his gaze rest on each precious face, the longest on Victoria's, imprinting every angle, every nuance, every beloved detail. "Goodbye," he said, his voice breaking on the last syllable.

Then he climbed into the car and waved as they called goodbye while he rode away. It was only as the car turned onto the highway that his brain replayed a single word.

Beloved? Victoria?

Absolutely beloved. But—

Good thing he was leaving. It would give him time to sort through the miasma of emotions roiling inside. And keep him from making promises he couldn't keep.

Chapter Thirteen

Without Ben, Victoria's days slid into weeks and turned into months of endless activities as a parade of young guests visited The Haven. While spring melted most of the mountaintop snowcaps, summer heat lent a lushness to the valley that quickly became the retreat her aunts had envisioned. Some were long-term guests. Some stayed a day or two, a weekend. Sullen, troubled kids who desperately needed care, kindness and most of all, love. Victoria strove to find a way to touch each heart. Most of those who visited left with a smile or at least happier than they'd arrived, proving that the aunties' vision of a refuge for foster kids was sorely needed.

Victoria got through the warm, busy days and the growing encumbrance of her pregnancy through prayer, through showering love on Mikey and leaning on the aunts and Darla. But mostly through trusting God. Time after time, she fought back her fear for Ben, refusing to admit how afraid she was to open the computer each night and find no word from him. Just a line or two, that's all she needed, she told herself. But what she craved was Ben's voice, his support, his reassurance. What she received were short, terse emails that said nothing about what he was doing.

For Mikey and the aunts' sake, she kept a brave face. And for Ben's. By tracking the news, she guessed he was involved in some type of rescue mission, as first one and then another compatriot of his was mysteriously "found." But her private fears mushroomed when his two-month absence turned into three, four, and then he no longer mentioned his return.

Caring for the aunts, raising Mikey and waiting for the birth of her child—all Victoria had to cling to was the same message she gave to the kids who came to The Haven: *Trust in the Lord with all your heart. Lean not on your own understanding.* Those words were how she chased away fear, how she clung to her hope for Ben and their future. She loved him—there was no point denying it. But whether he dared love her was another question.

"Victoria, come quickly," Tillie called. "Ben's on Facetime."

Weary from the late August heat and her pregnancy, heart in her throat with anticipation, Victoria moved as quickly as she could toward the study. Mikey was laughing and chatting with a shaggy-haired, bearded man who looked nothing like Ben. Then she heard that wonderful voice. For a moment, Victoria was content to just stand there and bask in relief.

Ben was okay.

"Is Victoria there?" His question snapped her back to awareness.

"I'm here." She moved into his sight line, aware of her ungainliness, messy hair and the ugly maternity dress she wore. What did they matter? "Hello, Ben." She forced down her tears. She might look awful but he wasn't going to see her cry. "How are you?"

"Better now that I see you." Lines around his eyes made him look tired. "You're so beautiful. How's the baby? Still kicking you at night?"

"Morning, noon and night," she responded before adding, "We've heard of a lot of fighting in your area." *Be fine,* she wished silently. *Come home.*

"I'm safe. Just tired of the heat and humidity."

They chatted for a while about inconsequential things like the weather and she realized they were alone. Still unable to voice the love she felt for him, Victoria told him about all the programs now fully operational at The Haven.

"Our activities are more successful than we even imagined. The kids get so worn out they're glad to relax. That's when they open up about their problems." Victoria savored every detail of his dear face, suddenly uncaring if he saw the love on hers. "The Haven's refuge is working, Ben. Kids are on a waiting list to come here. Even Thea and her sisters came for a weekend."

"I've been praying God would bless you." He fell silent. "I miss you, Victoria," he said in a much quieter voice. "I miss our walks and our discussions. I especially miss not being there to make sure you don't overdo it."

"I can't overdo it." She forced a laugh though her throat felt clogged with tears. "We have so many staff they'll hardly let me lift a finger." She hesitated before adding, "I miss you, too, Ben. Very much." She inhaled, forcing down the words of love she longed to say.

As Mikey's guardian, the military had sent her a letter emphasizing the need not to burden Ben with anything that could divert his attention from the work he had to do, though they'd not explained what that work was. Telling Ben she loved him would certainly divert his attention so Victoria kept mum.

"Another week or so and Mikey will be going to kindergarten." She wondered if Ben would be home for that.

"And you'll be having your baby," he whispered. "I'd hoped to be there in time for that but now—it's not looking good, Victoria."

"Darla's going to be my labor coach. I'll be fine. Don't worry about us. Take care of yourself." She had to stop, swallow and find her control before she could continue. "Folks at the seniors' center keep asking when you're coming back. They want you to start a weekly class with a different topic every week."

"Victoria," he paused, worry in his voice. "I don't know if I'll be able to stay and set up my store when I come back. I'm not sure there will be enough money for—"

"I've been thinking about that." She couldn't listen to why he couldn't stay nearby. She loved this man. She wanted him here so she could convince him that they had a future together.

"And?" his voice prodded her back to the subject at hand.

"Perhaps believing there isn't enough money for your start-up business is an excuse you're using so you won't have to take the chance. Maybe you really don't want it enough to risk it, Ben."

Maybe you don't want me.

Victoria waited for a response, but none came.

"There are loan programs available," she continued to fill in the silence, deliberately ignoring the military's letter now, for Mikey's sake and for her own. "Chokecherry Hollow has a special program to encourage new business. Do you truly want to open a computer store, Ben? Or is that another risk that's too big—like parenting Mikey? Like loving me?" she added very softly.

Ben was silent for several minutes, and then suddenly he had to go. Their goodbyes were rushed, not at all the way she wanted to end things. Victoria shut down Aunt Margaret's computer then went to sit on the patio to pray and to think.

But the baby kept kicking her in the ribs and the light lunch she'd eaten wasn't sitting right. On top of that, the questions circling inside her head were growing louder. Could Ben love her as she loved him or had his time in Africa broken the fragile bond they'd shared?

"Vic?" Mikey stood by her chair, his face thoughtful.

"What is it, sweetie?" He asked so little. Victoria thought she might resign herself to never having Ben's love if only he'd reconsider and take on parenting this precious child.

"Is God gonna let my Unca Ben die like He did my mommy and daddy?" One big fat tear coursed down each cheek.

"Oh, sweetheart." She lifted Mikey onto what remained of her lap and hugged him close. "God's with Uncle Ben just like He's here with us. Nothing's going to happen to your uncle without God's permission and you know who God is, don't you?"

"God is love," he said proudly.

"That's right, darling. I have an idea." Unable to give Mikey more reassurance because of the fear that gripped her, Victoria tried another tack. "I think we should plan a party for when Uncle Ben comes back."

"Okay." He jumped down, started toward the door. Then he turned around and studied her. "Will your baby be here then?"

"I'm not sure. Why?"

"Garnet said your baby is inside your tummy." Mikey's forehead pleated.

"That's right. Just like I explained." She waited. "Remember?"

"Yeah." Mikey frowned. "But how come you eated your baby, Vic?"

"What?" Startled, she gaped at him before bursting into laughter. "Why would you think that?"

"'Cause how'd it get there?" Mikey sighed. "Maybe you better 'splain 'bout babies again, Vic."

"Okay. Let's go get some lemonade first." As she walked toward the house, her heart brimmed with thanksgiving that she had a chance to love this dear child, but that was offset by the pain of not having Ben's love. *Oh, Lord, I'm trusting You to bring Ben home safely. But please, could You make him love me, too?*

Maybe it's an excuse—too big a risk—like loving me.

Victoria's words cycled through Ben's brain no matter how he tried to stuff them away.

"You got a girl back home?" Charley, the unit medic whose freedom Ben had bartered for just two hours ago, guzzled down more water then swiped his hand across his face, fully visible in the moonlight.

"Sort of." Was Victoria *his* girl? Yes!

"Wish I did. But lying in that hole for days on end, wondering if I'd die there made me realize something." Charley's eyes were bright in his dusty face. "I get home, I'm telling everyone I care about that I love them. Always kinda figured it wasn't necessary, that they knew. But I realized I haven't said 'I love you' to my mom in years. Nor Dad. How could they know?"

"Why haven't you told them?" Ben asked, curious about the reason.

"Seemed silly to go blabbing 'I love you.' Didn't want to take that risk, you know?" He shrugged, took another swig of water. "But you're dead, you never see them again, who cares if you looked silly? Some risks are worth it. You only get one life."

You only get one life.

The words resonated as Ben walked with him toward their camp. What if he didn't make it back? What if he died out here and Victoria never knew that he loved her? That he'd never felt as happy and complete as he did when he was with her? What if Mikey heard about his adoption plan and spent the rest of his life believing that Ben didn't love him?

"So you risk something and you fail. Or you get hurt. Or you mess up." Charley shook his head. "At least you did something with your life. You didn't just hide out and miss all the things you might have enjoyed. That's what I think." Charley grinned at the gatekeeper then clapped Ben on the shoulder. "Thanks a lot for getting me out, man."

"My pleasure."

"I need a shower. Then I'm calling my family. I got some things I gotta get said. Before it's too late." Charley hurried away.

After he'd been debriefed, Ben showered, too, before filling out tons of paperwork. It was quarter to seven in the morning by the time he'd finished. Too late to call home. The Haven—home?

Yes, it was. If home was where the heart was, The Haven deserved the name. But it was night there. And what could he say? "I can't come home yet because there's still a man missing?"

In a few hours, he'd head out again, try to find that man. But would he come back?

"I don't know what to do, God. I love Victoria. Have for ages. But I'm scared. It's not just her and me. There's Mikey and probably by the time I get back, she'll have her baby. I'll be responsible for a lot of people." That scared him.

But what was the alternative—life alone? That didn't bear thinking about.

Circular reasoning kept him going round and round until, out of sheer desperation, he grabbed his iPad and clicked on Neil's last journal, the only one he hadn't yet read.

Ben's always tried to be the father we never had. I sure didn't make it easy, but now I have my own son, I understand what he was up against. This kid, Mikey—I'm responsible for him and it's scary. He messes up, it's my fault. He makes the stupid choices I made—how do I stop him? I feel helpless just thinking about it. Poor Ben. What he must have gone through. But he stuck with me. No matter what I did to him, Ben was always there for me, trying to straighten me out, get me back on the right path. Because he loves me. It's only now, thinking about the future with Mikey, that I can begin to fathom how much he loved me. Enough to keep pushing me. Thank You, God, that Ben kept taking a chance on me.

Tears welled as Ben read his brother's words. They'd seldom talked about the past. Now he wished they had, that he'd known Neil's feelings. His gaze slid to the next paragraph.

Alice agrees with me—we're naming Ben as Mikey's guardian. If something happens to us, we both know Ben will do everything humanly possible for our son. That's the kind of man he is. Brave, courageous, fighting for what's right, no matter what. Ben doesn't run away from hard things. Responsibility is a trust he doesn't shirk. If he fails, he tries again. He'll help Mikey face the future because my big brother is an amazing man, worthy of our trust. I hope I can be even half of the man he is.

Doesn't shirk responsibility? Wasn't that exactly what he'd been trying to do with Mikey? Isn't that why he'd come up with the whole adoption idea—to escape his duty to the boy?

Ashamed, Ben bowed his head and prayed for forgiveness. Then a thought occurred. Was shirking what he was doing with his feelings for Victoria? Was he such a mouse that he ran away from love and all that it entailed? Was he afraid to be a father?

Yes!

Trust in the Lord with all your heart. Lean not

unto your own understanding. In all your ways acknowledge Him and He will direct your path.

Trust. That's all Ben had to do. Because God was in charge. Not him. God.

God had sent him Aunt Tillie and Margaret. And put Victoria there. God would take care of Mikey and Victoria's baby.

What in the world was he so afraid of?

Someone called his name.

"Major Adams, meet with the CO in ten minutes. Recon following."

"Has Jared, Sergeant Peel, been found?" Ben asked the soldier delivering the orders.

"Believe that's what the meeting's about, sir."

So he was going into harm's way again. Ben didn't hesitate. He pulled up his email account and shot off a note to Victoria. *I love you.*

Then he reported for duty, without fear, without hesitation.

Chapter Fourteen

For the first day in eons, The Haven did not have guests so the staff was taking a much-needed break. Even Tillie and Margaret had headed into Chokecherry Hollow for an afternoon of fun at the seniors' center, dropping Mikey at Garnet's.

Victoria hummed to herself as she wiped down the last of their newly delivered patio furniture, lovely wrought iron pieces that were answers to Jake's plea for replacement chairs that didn't require continual fixing. As usual, her thoughts turned to Ben. She hadn't heard from him in over a week.

"'Thou wilt keep him in perfect peace whose mind is stayed on'—ow!" She gasped, slowly straightened and laid a hand on her stomach. "I'm not really liking these—oh." The fierce cramping forced her to sit down and inhale.

Time passed and nothing more happened so

she resumed cleaning, admiring the look of the metal furniture on the weathered patio stones.

"Keep Ben safe, will you, Father?" she asked.

"Victoria."

That voice. She froze in place, unwilling to believe, certain it was a figment of her dreams.

"Aren't you going to speak to me?"

The voice was mixed up in her yearning for him and excruciating pain as her abdomen tightened again. She grasped a chair, sat down and slowly turned. Ben stood at the corner, holding a bunch of flowers.

"It's you," she whispered. "It's really you."

"In the flesh. Well, most of it. I got nicked by a bullet last week, but I'm fine and all the team is accounted for." He walked slowly toward her, limping just a little. "Are you all right?"

"I—ah—" Victoria was suddenly afraid, and the discomfort she was feeling didn't help. She licked her lips, her gaze riveted to him.

"Did you get my email?" he asked softly. She shook her head then squeezed her eyes closed as a much stronger sensation gripped her. He was by her side in a moment. "What's wrong, Victoria?"

"I'm very happy you're home, Ben. You belong here whether or not you know it. I thank God for answering my prayer. He's so trustworthy." She sucked in her breath and began counting, but she didn't get far before it started all over again. When his hand slid into hers, she grabbed it like a lifeline. "I'd love to sit and talk, my dear man, but I can't."

"You don't have to talk. There's just one thing I need to say." Ben inhaled but his gaze never left hers. "I love you, Victoria. Without you in it, my life is dull and boring. There's no fun left, no one to challenge me, to push me out of my rut." His beloved smile grew even more tender as his hand smoothed her hair. "You are a gift from God, one I desperately need. One I never want to do without. I love you, Victoria. Will you marry me?"

"Yes." It was the only word she could utter.

"Really?" Ben blinked. "No discussion, no comment about my stupidity in realizing it. No—"

"Maybe later." She stifled a groan as the pain increased. She huffed out a breath. "I love you, Ben. I promise I will say the vows you admire so much, the ones that promise I'll always be there, no matter what." She licked her lips, tried to smile. "But I have to do something else right now."

"What?" he demanded, obviously disgruntled to have his proposal upstaged.

"Have a baby." Victoria let out her breath as the cramp finally eased. "I love you very much, dear Ben. And I'm so glad you're safe and at home, but we need to go to the hospital."

"Now?"

Amused by the terror flooding his face, Victoria nodded.

"Right now. My bag is upstairs in my room. Would you get it, please? And hurry." If she hadn't been so busy practicing the breathing techniques she'd learned, she might have laughed at Ben's speed in retrieving her suitcase. Then he swung her into his arms and carried her to the car, flung her bag in the back and climbed into the driver's seat. "Your injury—" she protested.

"Is healed. Didn't you say Darla was your coach?" he demanded as they sped toward town. "Better call her."

"Good idea—oooh." Victoria breathed through the contraction until it lessened enough for her to slide her phone from her pocket and call her friend. "It's time," she said and then dropped the phone as pain engulfed her.

"Not far now, sweetheart," Ben soothed. After a sideways glance at her face, he pressed a little harder on the gas. "Keep breathing."

"It's kind of hard to stooooop," she wailed, hugely glad they'd arrived at the hospital.

Ben swept her into his arms and carried her inside without waiting for help.

"She's having a baby," he yelled at the nurse who came running. "Do something."

"Put her on this table," the nurse said calmly,

holding the curtain back. "And relax. Having a baby takes time."

"I don't think this little one knows that," Victoria told her, clinging to Ben's hand. "I'm pretty sure I have to push." When he tried to lessen her grip, she fixed him with a glare. "You're home now. You stay here," she ordered.

Ben's smile chased away all discomfort.

"I'm not going anywhere, darling Victoria. Not without you. This is where I belong, right by your side."

By Victoria's side was exactly where Ben remained while the nurse attended to her, relieved when the doctor arrived just in time to deliver a perfectly healthy little girl.

"Congratulations, Mommy," the nurse said as she set the baby on Victoria's chest. "What's her name?"

"Grace." Victoria smiled at Ben who thought she'd never looked more lovely. "Perfect, don't you think, darling? Because of God's grace to us."

"Absolutely perfect," he agreed right before he kissed her. That kiss went on and on until Darla burst into the room with Mikey and Garnet.

"Am I too late?" she gasped.

"You're just in time to meet Grace." Ben lifted up Mikey and then Garnet to see the new baby. "She's going to be your sister," he whispered to Mikey.

"How come, Unca Ben?" The boy looked at him so trustingly Ben's heart almost burst with love. He looked at Victoria.

"Because Victoria and I are getting married," he said, pausing just a moment to wait for her smile. "We're going to be a family."

"Oh." Mikey's little face screwed up as he struggled to puzzle it out. "So you're gonna be Unca Ben an' my dad?" he asked in confusion.

"I'll always be your Uncle Ben, Mikey. But I'd like to be your dad, too. If you want me to."

Victoria saw Ben's trepidation but she didn't worry. God had it all in hand.

"Yeah, I'd like to have a' Unca Dad," Mikey said with a huge grin.

Amid their laughter, Aunt Tillie stepped through the door followed by Aunt Margaret. They hugged Victoria then *oohed* and *ahhed* over little Grace, before embracing Ben. Tillie held out a box.

"You asked us to keep this for you, Ben. I think you probably want it now."

Ben smiled his thanks, opened the box and held up the robe he'd purchased for Victoria so long ago. "I bought this for you before Valentine's Day but was scared to give it to you."

"Did ya hear, Garnet? Unca Ben, uh, Dad, was scared."

Victoria fingered the delicate fabric then cupped her hand against his cheek.

"Thank you, darling." She suddenly realized they were alone. "I'd admired it in that window for days before our library trip with Thea. I wanted to buy it but thought it was too pretty for me. Then one day it wasn't in the window. I wondered who bought it."

"It's not quite pretty enough for you." Ben kissed her again. "I love you, Victoria Archer. When can we get married?"

She kissed him back with a laugh. "Can we wait a day? I'm a little tired."

"We can wait as long as you want," Ben said gallantly. "But not too long, okay? I want to be your husband."

"And I want to be your wife. But we have another group coming to The Haven the day after tomorrow, and then school starts. After that we'll be tied up with the weekend groups." Victoria frowned. "I'm not sure when—"

"I am." He grinned. "God will work it out. 'All things work together—'"

"'—for those who love God,'" Victoria finished. "We're going to have a wonderful life together building The Haven and watching God change lives. Aren't we, Ben?"

"Yep." After another kiss, Ben began to tell her his latest plans to develop The Haven so even more foster kids could find refuge and comfort.

When he realized Victoria and Grace had both

fallen asleep, he simply smiled and began making notes on the back of his plane ticket until the nurse came in and demanded he move his rental car.

"Would you mind asking someone else to do that?" Ben said. "It took me a long time to get home and now that I'm here, I'm not leaving." He glanced down at his family. "I've got a lot of responsibilities to attend to."

And he could hardly wait to get started.

With God's help.

* * * * *

Dear Reader,

Hi there! Welcome to The Haven, where God works things together to help His children. I love the Canadian Rockies. There's something about those craggy peaks and teal-blue lakes that reminds me that God is far bigger and more powerful than I can imagine.

Victoria needed to return to The Haven to recover her faith and trust in God—and in love. It wasn't easy, until she accepted that God loved her. Period. Not because she earned it but because God is love. Ben, too, struggled with acceptance of himself and his past failures. He feared parenting his nephew because he might fail again. It took him some time to realize that's why God's in charge.

I hope you'll return to The Haven for Adele's story. This good-natured chef wants a perfect family, but maybe perfect isn't part of God's plan for her life at all.

Blessings,

Lois Richer